Dead Are Alive

Dead Are Alive
The Heist
Copyright © 2012 Jason Thacker

First Edition

Dead Are Alive Edited By: Henry Snider
The Heist Edited By: John Lemut

Cover Art By: Jason Notter
Image Copyright Jason Notter 2012
Layout and Design: Scribe Imagery / Henry Snider

ISBN 10: 061565116X
ISBN13: 978-0615651163

First Printing: June, 2012

CONTENTS

Dead Are Alive

THE HEIST

Introduction

Zombies man, they totally don't creep me out. I love those hungry, rotting corpses and all they represent. There are loads of different types of zombie tales. There's the traditional Romero style slow movers and their endless numbers wiping out the human race. There's books about superheroes taking on the walking dead, zombies in space, and zombies fighting other monsters like vampires, werewolves, and even Bigfoot. Zombies work in just about any time period or plot. . .But one of the coolest places to find zombies is the Old West. The Old West was a "survival of the fittest" kind of world anyway and zombies just bring that out even more. A well written zombie western can get the heart pumping like few other things can. Joe R. Lansdale wrote what was perhaps one of the greatest with Dead in the West and numerous others have followed in his wake. Whole anthologies of western zombie tales have made their way to print such as "The Zombist" from Library of the Living Dead Press. I've even played around with a twisted version of the concept myself with my book The Weaponer.

The western itself seems to be making a comeback and with it, the number of zombie infested ones continue to grow. Action packed tales of the walking dead mixed with blazing guns, horses, and well done character development- That's what Jason Thacker delivers here. Thacker doesn't pull his punches with the horror either. Expect some chills and a few moments where you spring out of your seat, cheering for the heroes. Dead Are Alive is a zombie western with teeth. It's not a book you'll easily put down and you'll find yourself telling your friends about it long after the last page is turned.

Eric S Brown - Author of the Bigfoot War series

Dead Are Alive

Prologue

Percy McAndrews would normally be a drunken mess after a fishing trip at the river, or at any other time for that matter, but this hadn't been his normal empty-handed trip. He proudly carried ten fish on a string over his shoulder. Percy's mouth watered at the thought of the fish sizzling in a frying pan later that night. It would be the biggest dinner he'd ate in quite some time. He whistled as he walked across the wooded ridge top on the way back home to Hazel. A soft breeze blew through his white, dirty hair and scruffy, white beard. Water still dripped from the fish and drenched the back of his blue, button-up shirt. Percy's brown, tattered pants, rolled up to the knees, revealed his scrawny legs. The grass felt cool against his bare feet; a more welcomed feeling compared to the sharp, pointed rocks he crossed down by the river.

Percy came to a sudden stop when he heard what sounded like a woman's scream. He stood still as the scream once again echoed up from the small grassy meadow right below. Percy ran behind a large tree that overlooked the meadow. Four men stood in a circle around another man, who tugged on an old woman's hair as she lay face down on the ground.

"Come on, granny! Scream so the whole town can hear!" said the tall, muscular man as he pulled the woman's long, gray hair even harder. Percy recognized the woman as her head snapped back. It was Reverend Hopkins' wife, Gwen.

Percy whispered to himself, "What are they doing with the Reverend's wife out here?" He nervously licked his lips and glanced all around. "I gotta help her." Percy took a step from the tree. "Who am I kidding? They'd stomp me into the ground. I need help." He eased back into hiding.

The man leaned down and forcefully kissed Gwen on her lips. Her screams continued to echo through the woods. He held Gwen under the chin as she struggled to move her face away. The other men cheered like savages as Gwen begged the man to stop.

Suddenly the man jumped up as he shouted, "She bit me! The old hag about bit my lip off!" Percy was close enough to see the blood running down the muscle-man's chin. Gwen tried to crawl away.

Another man with a long scruffy beard laughed as he said, "I don't blame her, who'd wanna kiss you anyways?" He walked over, grabbed one of Gwen's legs, and pulled her back to him. "Where you think you're going, woman? I think you need to be taught a lesson in manners."

The muscular man smiled with his bloody teeth. "Teach her!"

All five of them ganged up and started kicking Gwen all over her body. She screamed in agony as the men relentlessly pummeled her.

"That's it. This has gotta stop." said Percy as he started toward the gang. Just as Percy stepped from behind the wide tree, he noticed a large man on a horse approaching them. Percy took cover once again and watched the horse come closer to the group. Percy squinted his eyes.

"Uh-oh boys. You're in for it now. That's Sheriff Wellman coming."

Sheriff Wellman was known for the noticeable attire he always wore. He had on a bright red jacket and matching vest over a white shirt. His black pants matched the leather hat on his head. He kept a thick, neatly trimmed, gray mustache that ran all the way down to his chin.

The men finally stopped their attack as the horse came to a stop. Percy saw the anger on Sheriff Wellman's face.

Wellman looked at each of the men in disgust as he said, "What do you idiots think you're doing?" The men looked at each other, embarrassed.

Gwen could barely move, she gasped for air as she whimpered, "Sheriff. Thank goodness."

Just then, the man with the hooked-nose spoke up in a raspy voice, "We were just having a little fun, Sheriff. Don't be mad." He seemed to be the leader.

Sheriff Wellman threw his hands in the air. "Fun? I thought I was clear when I last spoke with you boys."

The hook-nosed man looked around at his other comrades, then down at Gwen, who still struggled to get to her feet. "Sheriff, we didn't do anything wrong. We did what you asked."

Sheriff Wellman rolled his eyes as he shook his head. "You moron. I specifically told you not to get caught!" He pointed down at Gwen. "That right there is Reverend Hopkins' wife!"

The leader bit his bottom lip. "Well, she was there when we got inside. We had to bring her with us or else we'd been caught for sure."

Wellman gritted his teeth as he looked to the sky and mumbled curse words. The men stood there and looked at their leader uneasily.

"So when do we get our pay for this, Sheriff?" asked

the man. Gwen managed to rise to her knees, and struggled to stand up. Sheriff Wellman watched as he seemed to think of an answer for the man.

"Shew," said Wellman as he reached down for the pistol hanging from his belt. He drew it from the holster and fired one quick shot at Gwen. Blood sprayed as she instantly fell limp and hit the ground.

Percy felt a cold chill rush down his spine as he watched Gwen's body collapse. "What?" His body started to shake. "Why in the world would Sheriff Wellman kill Gwen?"

As Wellman placed his gun back into its holster he asked, "Now where's the money?"

The hook-nosed leader looked to the shortest one of the men and nodded. The short man untied a cloth bag from the saddle on his horse and handed it up to Wellman.

"I suspect all of it's here?" asked Wellman.

The leader nodded. "Of course it's there, Sheriff. Now when do we get to see our part of it?"

Wellman placed the rugged cloth bag inside a brown, leather saddlebag. "When the job's done." The men seemed confused. "Get rid of her and we'll talk payment. I can't have the blood of the preacher's wife on my hands along with a church robbery. Meet me at the jailhouse around noon tomorrow; unless she hasn't disappeared. I don't want to see none of you until then!"

The men looked at Wellman with long faces. Their leader replied, "Sure thing, Sheriff. We'll see you tomorrow at noon then."

Wellman turned his horse around as he said, "Don't get caught this time!" He started on his way back toward Hazel as the men dragged Gwen's lifeless body across the ground.

Percy dropped his fish and ran in the other direction.

His heart pounded as he started to envision the men catching up to him and killing him too. Percy knew he needed to tell somebody about what just happened, but with the sheriff involved, he wasn't sure who.

Chapter 1

The summer sun rose near its zenith, and heat bore down on everything in Hazel. Sweat from Fred Douglas' hand coated the sidearm's ivory handle as he awaited the arrival of Sheriff Wellman. His round leather hat concealed a thatch of short, dark-brown hair that ran from the crown of his head down to a thin unshaven beard. Fred often did this for personal gain, but this time was different. He only wanted to do this to make things right.

At last the door of Hazel's jailhouse swung open. Two men stood there as they held the large steel door wide open. One of them bore a long scruffy beard, and the other had no teeth. Next followed two more men. The first was tall and very muscular; the next was the shortest with a dark mustache.

That's him. Fred readied his gun. He opened the cylinder on the Colt .45. Six shots ready to bark at the desired target. The reasons for killing Wellman would be justified soon after.

A bold voice coming from just inside the door of the jailhouse said, "Glad we were able to get that took care of gentlemen. Now, I'm goin' after me some lunch." Out stepped a man dressed in a black jacket and vest over a bright red shirt. Pants and boots matched the solid ebony vest. He placed a black top hat with a striped red and ebony ring of fabric near the bottom, atop his head. He held a gold pocket watch in one hand, chain glimmering in the sunlight as he checked the time of day. Wellman placed it back inside his breast-pocket and pulled the jacket back in place. A bit of lint marred his sheriff's badge. Hazel was a medium-sized town, so there wasn't any need to have a lot of political figures oversee the town. Wellman served as both mayor and sheriff to Hazel.

A hook-nosed man followed the sheriff as he stepped out of the doorway. He said in a raspy voice, "Now you make sure to let us know if you ever need anything again, Sheriff. We'll be happy to oblige."

They proceeded down the dusty street with Wellman in the middle. The muscular man and the short one led, with the toothless man and bearded guy following. Their hook-nosed leader brought up the rear.

"Six of 'em. Just like Percy said." thought Fred, "These shots are gonna have to count." Using his back, Fred pushed himself forward from the building he leaned against, calmly walked out from the alleyway and out into the street. With two quick bursts of gunfire Fred dropped the first two of the gang. Fred sped up to a run and slid behind a horse-water trough. The sheriff and three remaining members of the gang stumbled back, fumbling for their guns. Another shot rang from Fred's pistol, and with it the toothless man fell, clinching his chest. People panicked and ran for cover. The sheriff and the other two men ran into an alley.

"Who was that?" demanded Sheriff Wellman as he shook the gang's leader by the shirt collar.

"I don't know! I swear I don't!"

"I think it was Fred Douglas." said the bearded man as he drew his own pistol.

"Fred Douglas! Ooh boys, I tell you," said Wellman as he pushed the hook-nosed leader away. "I knew I should've had him thrown away to rot a long time ago!" Just then, the sheriff leaned out and fired off a shot in Fred's direction.

"Where's he at?" questioned the bearded man.

"He's over there by the watering trough!" Wellman fired another shot in that direction.

The bearded man leaned out for a glimpse at his target. His eyes wandered around the town frantically in hopes of catching any sign of Fred's whereabouts.

"Do you see him?" nervously asked the gang leader.

Silence.

Only the sound of the wind blowing through the streets reached the bearded man's ears. He turned away from the breeze to listen for the gunslinger. Suddenly a loud thump came from the trough just outside of the mill, shattering the heavy silence.

"He's over there!" shouted the man as he ran out of the alley. He fired the pistol toward the sound with rage seen only in those consumed with the desire to kill.

Fred rose up from the water trough across the street from the one the bearded man marched toward. Fred used a rock as a decoy to lure the henchman in that direction. Fred aimed and fired. Blood sprayed as the bullet tore through the man's side and exited out his heart. He fell limp and collided to the ground with a thud.

Without hesitation, Fred walked toward Sheriff Wellman at a steady pace. The dust from the streets swept about in a massive cloud by gusty wind. Fred's long black trench coat danced in the wind as its tail flowed behind. With the gun lowered, he walked toward the sheriff. Wellman still cowered alongside the hook-nosed gang leader in the alleyway.

Sheriff Wellman screamed, "Where's he at? What's going on?" He shook the gang leader by the arm.

"I don't know Sheriff, I don't know. He done killed everybody else!"

"Look and see, you idiot!" demanded Wellman and pushed the man to the corner of the building. Hesitant, the hook-nosed man eased toward the edge of the old wooden structure; its boards were rigid and weathered. The man placed his hands softly on the wall's surface. His whole body shook. Hooknose's knees began to buckle under the weight of his own body. Fear consumed him. With the ounce of courage left in his soul, the man forced himself to look beyond the safety the alleyway held.

A flash of light, then darkness.

The last man fell to the ground. The extra bullets in the small cloth sack attached to his belt jingled as they spilled out onto the dirt. Fred marched into the alley toward the sheriff. Wellman fell to his knees and clumsily tried to cock the hammer on his pistol. Shaky, sweat-covered hands slipped. Fred rushed the sheriff and kicked the gun from his hands.

The sheriff stared straight down the barrel of the still-smoking gun. Tears poured down Wellman's face. The neatly trimmed mustache drenched with snot that oozed from his nose. The sheriff's face reddened as sweat beaded on his brow.

"Why?" uttered Sheriff Wellman.

"Why? Let me ask you Sheriff, why cry now?" asked Fred. "Is it because your men are all dead?" Fred paused as he looked around. "No? Well, is it because all of this town's people are inside hiding and no one is here to help you?" Fred paused once again for an answer as he looked into Wellman's tear-filled eyes. "Still no? I know! It's cause you're missing lunch right about now, ain't it?

You're missing stuffing your fat face with all the food you can." Fred eased closer to Wellman's face. "Ohh, licking any bit off of your fingers and smacking your lips while your mouth fills with all that good taste. Mmm I bet it is." He waited for any answer from the sheriff. "Ain't it!" demanded Fred as he pushed the barrel of the gun against the cheek of Wellman's face.

"Nooo." cried Wellman. His emotions pushed over the breaking point.

Fred laughed. "What a man we have here. What a man!" Continuing to aim his gun at Wellman's face, Fred turned to yell to everyone in town. "Look here, it's the mayor and sheriff of Hazel, everybody! Good ol' Sheriff Wellman! The same man who stole the money from the church and killed Reverend Hopkins' wife!"

Sheriff Wellman's emotions slid from fear to rage. "What! You're a liar Fred! You don't know nothin' about anything like that! I swear I'll have you killed for doing this!" said Wellman.

Fred knelt before Wellman and calmly said, "You ain't got nobody left to kill me, Sheriff." Fred chuckled at the situation.

Sheriff Wellman pointed at Fred with a shaky hand, but remained on his knees and said, "You ain't no man neither, Fred. If you didn't have that gun pointed at me you wouldn't be nothing."

Fred stopped for a second. With a stern look, he lowered his revolver from the sheriff's face. Wellman's eyes followed the barrel and a sense of relief washed over. Fred smiled and made a quick kick right under Wellman's chin, knocking him back. Fred readied his gun once again.

"How about that? You ain't just fat, you're stupid too," Fred said with a chuckle.

Blood poured from the sheriff's mouth. He spat two

bloody teeth to the ground knocked out by the blow.

"Too bad you're not gonna live to remember this lesson, Sheriff." Fred prepared to fire the final bullet left in his gun. "Don't take stuff that don't belong to you. I don't like it."

Fred was knocked off his feet. The gun fell from his hand and landed several feet away. The sheriff rolled away from the two men as they struggled with one another. The only thing Wellman managed to do was sit, catch his breath, and watch. Wellman immediately recognized his savior and let out a great battle cry,

"Get him Deputy, get him!"

It was Sheriff Wellman's goodhearted sidekick, Deputy Sid Hansen. The deputy scuffled with Fred on the dusty ground. His clean-cut brown hair became mangled as Fred tried to put him in a headlock. Deputy Hansen managed to wiggle his slightly built physique and free himself from Fred's hold. When standing straight, the deputy stood around six-foot tall. He wore old, worn-out jeans, a red button-up shirt with the sleeves rolled up past the elbows. Deputy Hansen once again charged Fred, knocking him back to the ground. Dust now covered the black leather vest over Sid's shirt.

The deputy wrestled Fred around to his belly and held the gunslinger's hands behind and struggled to place handcuffs around Fred's wrists. Once locked, Deputy Hansen raised himself to his feet. Fred lay there, tasting dust in his mouth as he tried to spit. The grit on his teeth felt almost as uncomfortable as the agonizing pressure of Deputy Hansen's boot in his back.

"I see you've been busy while I've been gone." said Deputy Hansen to Wellman as he put his hand out to help the sheriff up off the ground.

"Nothing a good hangin' won't fix." Sheriff Wellman kicked Fred in the ribs. "Not that I'm complaining or anything, but what are you doing back so soon?"

Deputy Hansen dusted his vest off and said, "Well, I stopped by the doctor's house on my way out to Whittlersfield, but nobody was home."

"I guess he was out on a visit." commented Sheriff Wellman as he tried to rub the soreness out of his neck.

Deputy Hansen continued with a distraught look, "Must've had a few people to see, he wasn't there when I got back either. I still got all the supplies he asked me to pick up loaded in the wagon."

"Ah, just leave it at the jail for now," said Wellman as he dusted his sleeve.

Fred's head pounded like a herd of wild stallions galloping on an open range as he laid there lifeless. Blood trickled from his nose and his left eye already began to swell.

"Bring him on." Wellman said and gathered himself, placing the hat back on. He walked over and dusted off Fred's gun.

Fred felt the deputy tug the back of his shirt and pull him to his feet. The gunslinger staggered in whichever direction the deputy led him. Everyone abandoned their hiding places to catch a glimpse of the prisoner.

The sheriff proudly led Deputy Hansen and their newest capture toward the jailhouse. Onlookers stared as they talked amongst each other.

"That's Fred Douglas." said an older woman to her husband.

"It sure is, ain't it." confirmed her slack-jawed spouse as he watched the trio walk by.

The closer they got to the jailhouse, the louder voices grew. Whispers turned to quiet chatter, which were soon overpowered by frantic ramblings of dismay. Just as they reached the door of the adobe fortress, a brave man with a tobacco stained beard ran to them yelling,

"Hey! Hey, Sheriff wait!" The men stopped just before they entered the jailhouse. Wellman turned to the man already in anticipation of the question about to follow.

"Yes? May I help you, sir?" asked Wellman in an arrogant and boastful voice.

"Why are you taking-in Fred?" asked the man as he caught his breath.

"For the murder of five innocent men and also attempted murder, my friend!" declared the sheriff with a firm stare.

The man wore a confused expression on his face and said, "Attempted? What do you mean?"

"I mean he tried to kill me! In cold blood!" said Wellman in a dramatic voice as he patted his own chest.

With a sheepish smirk the man replied, "Well let me tell you, Sheriff, you're one lucky guy."

Sheriff Wellman raised an eyebrow and asked, "How so?"

"Cause Fred never lets his man get away. And if they ever did get away, well, Fred just never will give up." The man squinted his eyes and hunkered his head between his shoulders. "He's like an old coon dog. He's tenacious. He'll sniff ya out till he's got ya up a tree. Then that's when he lowers the boom on ya! Bam!" He slammed his fist into his other hand. "You're caught. Might as wells say it's over," the man said with excitement usually reserved for children describing a hero. The sheriff stood there, face flushing with anger. Fred watched the sheriff, then lowered his head and shook it. Fred knew the man didn't help the current situation any.

Wellman slowly nodded. "Well that's why we're gonna hang him high in the street. Just so everybody can see, Fred Douglas ain't the one that always gets his man; it's me." The sheriff once again patted his chest. "Sheriff Wellman!"

"What!? You can't do that!" pleaded the man. He nervously looked to Fred. "Why'd you do it for, Fred?"

With his head still hung, Fred uttered, "He stole everybody's money and killed–" Wellman slugged Fred right in the mouth.

"He's a liar!" The sheriff shook his hand and held it, trying to numb the pain. Wellman turned back to the distraught man who was stunned by the sudden outburst.

"S-sorry to have bothered you, Sheriff. Have a good day," stuttered the man as he nervously walked away.

Not many people were used to Wellman losing his cool in that way. However, the one man used to the outbursts was Sid Hansen, who still stood there, embarrassed by the sheriff's public flare-up. Most of the time, the outbursts occurred behind closed doors. When the sheriff did have these public occurrences, Deputy Hansen was forced to go on damage control. Wellman didn't want the people of Hazel to think of him as anything except an outstanding leader of their town.

Realizing he may have went a little overboard just then, Wellman calmly said, "Let's get inside."

With one hand on Fred, Hansen opened the door to Hazel's jailhouse. Two oak desks sat against the far wall. The walls were the same dirty orange color as the outside. Rugged, wooden boards covered the floor. A scent of damp dirt filled the air inside the desolate room. The sheriff went straight to his cluttered desk, took off his gun holster and laid it amongst the mess. Wellman sat down on the thick pillow in the seat.

As he propped his feet on the desktop, Wellman said, "Put him where I can keep an eye on him." He leaned over, opened the bottom desk drawer and pulled out a bottle of whiskey. Deputy Hansen led Fred to one of the four unoccupied cells. They lined the back of the room. Fred was led to the cell directly across from Wellman's desk. The deputy got the keys which hung on a rusty spike in the wall next to the sheriff's desk. With a quick turn of the key and a push, the heavy iron door swung open with a grating moan from the hinges. Inside the cell rested a bed barely big enough for a grown-man. A green, ratty blanket covered the thin, so-called mattress. Both the blanket and mattress were covered in stains. A foul odor wafted from them.

"Lovely accommodations," thought Fred. He stood there admiring his cell's décor as the deputy removed his handcuffs. Then the same annoying squeak came from behind him as the door swung shut.

"Well, that's that." said the sheriff. He placed his palms on the desk and pushed himself up from the chair. "I'm heading back out to Betty's to get something to eat. Stay here and watch our celebrity for me, Deputy."

"Sure thing." replied Deputy Hansen with a nod.

Fred watched Sheriff Wellman as he strutted out the door and headed to the only restaurant in town. The jailhouse door swung closed. Hansen corked the sheriff's whiskey and put it back into the bottom drawer.

"You always clean up Wellman's messes?"

Hansen let out an aggravated sigh as he shut the drawer. "Look, Fred, I was just doing my job. That's all."

"Oh, hey, don't get all testy with me, Sid. Just wondering if you've got any extra in there for me." The sarcasm seethed. "Don't put it away so quick."

"Fred, I know what you meant by that." He walked to the front of Wellman's desk. "Really, what was I supposed to do?"

Fred stared at him a moment then noted, "And do you think Wellman would ever jump in and save the day for you like that?"

"Well–"

"The answer is no, Sid. No. He wouldn't." Fred

pointed at Sid. "Your sheriff is a coward. He thinks only of himself. He wouldn't care if everyone and thing in this town was wiped out. As long as he still called the shots, have all the money and booze still coming in to him, he wouldn't care. That's just the bottom line of it all. He don't care."

Sid walked over by Fred's cell and leaned against the jail's cold walls.

"Look, it wasn't anything personal, you and me go way back. Besides, I've got a wife and kid at home, they depend on me, and I depend on this job to take care of them."

Fred shook his head in bewilderment, and turned it toward one of the cell walls; wondering how his plan had gone so wrong.

Still puzzled by Fred's actions, Sid asked, "What's going on anyways, Fred?"

Fred kicked the wall. He cuffed his hands together as he hunched over and sat on the bed. With elbows on knees he remained despondent and looked down at the filthy floor beneath him. With a heavy sigh Fred answered, "He robbed the money that Reverend Hopkins was taking up to expand the church and murdered Reverend Hopkins' wife, Gwen."

"Do what? Fred, where'd you hear something like that from?"

"Percy McAndrews." stated Fred as he looked down at the ground. He continued, "He was on his way back home yesterday after fishing down at the river. He saw those five men beating Gwen to death. Wellman rode in on his horse and was pretty mad about Gwen being there. Percy said the gang's leader told Wellman she was there when they went in to rob the church. They kidnapped her and took her into the woods where they met Wellman." Fred raised his head and looked Sid in the eyes. "Wellman shot her right there. One of the men gave him a bag of money and asked about their share. Wellman told them to get rid of Gwen's body and meet him here, today at noon."

"Fred, are you sure? You and me both know Percy likes to drink. You think he may have just been having one of his moments?" asked Deputy Hansen as he scratched the back of his neck.

Fred shook his head, "I thought the same thing when he first came to me with this. This time was different. Percy was really shaken up by it. The man wasn't drunk, Sid. Believe me."

"Gwen must have been doing some cleaning and getting the church ready for the services." Sid shook his head. "But why was she in there yesterday? Don't she usually wait until Saturday to clean?"

"She was supposed to go out of town with the reverend today to see if anybody would wanna donate to the church. She went in after school was over to get the cleaning done a day early, and that's where Wellman's plan turned sour. Nobody was supposed to be there at that time."

Sid put his hands in his pockets, "Did Reverend Hopkins tell anyone Gwen was missing?"

"Maybe. You were out of town this morning, so the only lawman he could have told is Wellman. I'm guessing the sheriff didn't tell you nothing about it." assumed Fred.

Sid looked around as he thought for a second, then straightened. "No. I even talked to him before I left this morning." confirmed Sid.

Fred clapped his hands once. "That's what I thought! I heard for myself that Gwen went missing yesterday. Wellman isn't about to have anybody start looking for her cause he knows exactly what happened to her."

Sid nervously said, "Fred, nobody is gonna believe

this. He's a well-respected man, everybody trusts him."

Fred was quick to ask, "You included?"

"I'm not so sure anymore." Sid's expression gave away his new feeling of insecurity for the sheriff.

"That's what I figured. Go see for yourself, Sid. You don't have to just take my word for it. I wouldn't blame you if you did go to check it out." said Fred in a rational tone. "I mean, you're probably gonna need Percy to tell you for himself anyways."

Sid nodded, "Yeah you're right. I need to have a witness that actually seen it all happen before anything can really be done–legally anyway."

Fred grinned. "I guess I skipped a few steps."

Sid shook his head. "Shew, I tell you what. I'm gonna go to Percy's house and see if he will agree to be a witness against the sheriff, and maybe get a few more details from him." He moved to his desk and took a small piece of paper from the top drawer. "I'll just be gone a little while Fred. You need anything while I'm gone?"

Fred stretched his neck to look at Deputy Hansen's desk. "Yeah, hand me that Bible over there sitting on your desk."

"You know that book front to back already, don't you?" Sid picked it up from his desk and walked toward Fred's cell. "You know everybody wonders about you. They don't understand how you can carry your Bible around with you, always show up for church services, but still go around and kill all those people." Sid handed his Bible to Fred through the iron bars. "I'm not saying none of those people didn't deserve what was coming to them. If you ask me, I think it's a good thing you do what you do."

Fred held the Bible up and winked. "Thanks old pal. You'd better get to moving."

Sid made his way to the door and hurried out, on his

way to find Percy.

* * *

An hour or so after leaving, Sid made his way through the sturdy door once again.

"Still think Percy was just seeing things?" questioned Fred with his eyes locked on the gospel, his words full of sarcasm.

Sid sat down in his chair and stared at the blank sheet of paper in his hand. "This is bad, Fred. Percy skipped town."

Fred's eyes looked away from the words and toward Sid. "Where did he go?"

Sid leaned forward in his chair. "Percy's neighbors said, after he heard you were arrested, he just packed up a few things and headed for Whittlersfield."

"I guess he got spooked." Fred closed the Bible and laid it next to him.

"He probably figured the sheriff would find out he told you, and then have somebody come after him next." Sid looked out the window, past the iron bars toward Betty's Restaurant. "What in the world would make Sheriff Wellman kill Gwen and take that money?"

"Well, about the money, my guess would be food by the looks of him."

"Seriously, Fred, what am I gonna do?" Sweat beaded on Sid's forehead as he fidgeted with a pen. He looked at the pendulum clock hanging on the wall. "I don't know, it's already after seven. Sheriff Wellman has probably already gone home for the day. It'll be night before long anyways, I'll just have to head back up to Whittlersfield tomorrow and find Percy. I'll have to try and get a little rest tonight." Sid got up from his chair and made his way towards Fred's cell. "Sorry about everything today, old buddy. I didn't know."

Fred shrugged his shoulders. "Ah, it's alright; I know you gotta do your job. You just go on home and take care of that wife and youngin of yours . I'm sure they're getting worried and wondering where you're at." assured Fred.

Sid bit his bottom lip. "Alright, Fred, I'll be back in the morning. Wellman hardly ever shows up on a Sunday."

"I'll see ya, Sid."

"See ya." Sid closed and locked the door behind him.

Chapter 2

Just beyond the canyon walls and swirling dust clouds that surrounded this typical western town, was a land of tranquil beauty. The barren desert gave-way to large fields of green grass. The earth itself resembled massive waves created by a rolling sea. Sparse trees along the land transformed into lush forests. Gentle streams and mighty rivers slithered their way throughout the landscape like veins coursing through a body. Game and wildlife were abundant in this area. This is where most of the locals and visitors alike enjoyed a peaceful evening away from the busy streets of Hazel.

The sound of running water and an occasional animal call filled the air. Paradise was quiet and calm as usual. A large flock of birds seemed to explode from the branches of a towering oak tree as the shriek of a child disrupted the calmness.

"Ahhhh! Help! Help! Somebody please!" screamed the child. Laughter, contrasting the pleas, erupted. It echoed from three children and two adults.

"I've got you now little boy! You're mine!" said an adult male. "Gotcha, gotcha, gotcha!" The children shrilled and cackled as the man chased them around the field.

"Margret, can you come give Mommy a hand real quick?" said a woman.

"Sure, Mama." said the little girl. She ran up the grassy knoll to her mother.

"Come on boys, let's go help your mother and sister." said the man, motioning for them.

"Alright, Daddy." said one of the two boys as they ran to him.

The man picked up Donald, the younger of the two, and put him on his shoulders as he followed the other boy, Timmy up the hill.

"Well, well. Looks like someone decided to do a little work today," she jokingly commented to her husband.

"Now, Gloria, you know I'm not going to pass up a beautiful day like this and spend some time with my family." said the man. "Besides, nobody came by today. Not that many people get sick during the summer around here."

Dr. Gene Richards closed the practice up early today to go on a picnic with his wife and three kids.

"Daddy, why do people get sick?" asked little Donald, who still sat atop Gene's shoulders.

"Cause, Donald. Sometimes these little tiny bugs get inside of us." Gene reached over his head and put his hands under Donald's arms to lower him to the ground.

As Donald's feet touched the dark green grass he asked, "Bugs?"

Dr. Richards knelt down to eye level with Donald. "Well not like the kind we see. These bugs are so tiny you can't even see them. That's how people get sick. Those bugs crawl right up on you and go right up your nose!" said Gene as he gently grabbed Donald's nose between his two fingers. Everyone let out a collective chuckle as Donald squirmed and giggled.

"Honey, when you're done scaring the children would you care to put these blankets in the wagon?" asked Gloria as she folded the last one.

"Scaring the children?" the doctor asked as he walked to her. "They know there's nothing to be scared of. People come to me to get better my dear."

Gloria smiled at her husband as she handed him an armful of folded blankets. Gene turned and made his way to their horse-drawn wagon. Close behind followed the boys. Gloria and Margret gathered the dishes and placed them into the picnic basket.

"Daddy, can me and Donald go throw rocks in the river?" asked Timmy as Gene put the blankets in the back of the wagon.

"Yeah, but you boys better be careful, and keep an eye on your brother." said Gene. He continued, "But hurry. It'll be getting dark before long; so only for a few minutes."

"Alright, Dad." said an excited Timmy. "Come on Donald." The boys ran into the small wooded area toward the river.

"Where are we going?" He ran close behind his older brother.

"Down to the river to throw rocks." He pushed a small limb out of his path.

The duo made their way through the trees as they stepped over logs and climbed across small boulders. Timmy forged his way through the thick netting of green pine needles and small maple saplings with his brother in tow. Soon the dense coverage of the forest gave-way to a large, calm section of river. Scattered all along the edge of the glassy, green water laid thousands of rocks ranging in size.

"Come on Donald!" insisted Timmy as he quickened his pace toward the water's edge. The two rushed to grab a rock small enough to ensure the maximum distance possible across the deep water. Donald was the first to launch his best throw. With a small splash; the calmness of the water's surface began to ripple in small waves that raced away from the sinking rock. Challenged to outclass his brother's throw; Timmy drew back as far as he could–took a giant step forward, and threw his rock with all of his might. The two stared in amazement as the stone rocketed through the air. When it finally met with the water; it traveled nearly triple the distance of Donald's attempt.

"How do you throw that far?" asked an amazed Donald.

"Don't know. I just throw it as hard as I can." replied Timmy as he was looking for another rock.

Confident in his skills–Timmy reached for another rock about the same size as the first. The boys continued to amuse themselves for a few more throws.

"Alright, that's enough." said Timmy. "Mom and Dad are probably ready to go. We better head back now."

Trying to make his last one count; Donald threw his final attempt with unsatisfactory results.

"You'll get it one day." said Timmy as he tried to encourage his younger brother.

Donald looked up to Timmy a lot. Everything Timmy did–Donald mimicked. Timmy knew this and tried his best to be a role model for Donald. He always helped him out, and looked after him. The two began to walk back toward the picnic site. Once again they pushed away tree limbs and scaled over the same small boulders they did on their way to the river. Their pace was much slower than that of their journey in. With the extra time given by their slow departure from the riverside; Timmy and Donald found time to take in the sights and sounds of their surroundings. Donald, the curious seven year-old, had a tendency to wander off and become easily distracted. Something caught his attention.

"Donald, we ain't got time to look around. We gotta get back." said Timmy as Donald made a cautious stride toward a curious object. "Donald! Mom and Dad are gonna be mad!" anxiously demanded Timmy.

Donald approached a grey oval mass. It appeared bigger than one of his mother's iron skillets and hung from a low limb. Its fibers were woven in a mangled frenzy of torn leaves and dead grass. A thin, twig-like stem was all that held the strange apparatus from falling to the earth below.

"Timmy... look!" said Donald in awe of this magnificent creation just feet from where he stood.

"Get back!" yelled Timmy. "That looks like a hornet's nest!"

"Nuh-uh!" exclaimed Donald as his face lit up with excitement. Just like his father; Donald held a great fascination in insects. He and his father spent hours hunting and examining any species of insect they found. So, naturally, Donald first searched for a long stick.

"Donald! Are you crazy?" yelled Timmy.

Close by lay a branch long enough for Donald's intent.

Timmy anticipated Donald's next move. "Hey, Donald, don't be stupid! I swear you'd better not!" Donald stepped as far back as he could and pointed the stick at the nest "Stupid! Quit it! I'm serious!"

"Shh!" demanded Donald as he stuck his tongue out the side of his mouth and squinted his eyes in a stare of deep concentration. The blunt end stick crept closer to the nest.

"Oh my gosh, what an idiot! He's really going to." whispered Timmy as he turned to begin a mad dash to distance himself even further from Donald and the nest.

Donald tried to keep complete attention on the stick he held. It brushed against the surface of the grey shell.

Donald began to rock it back and forth. Timmy stood in utter horror as he watched his younger brother from a distance of no less than fifty-feet. The hive remained calm. Donald, who was then more certain of himself than ever before took two steps forward. Again he gently pressed the stick against the hive; he increased the intensity of the pressure behind his shoves. Donald noticed the small brownish-red particles that fell from the hole on the bottom of the nest. A rush of terror raced through his whole body as his eyes fell downward as the nest plummeted from the branch which held it. Upon impact the grey mass crunched as it hit the soil.

"Donald! Run!" screamed Timmy from afar, but it was too late–Donald already dropped the stick and turned toward Timmy's way. Donald didn't look back; he just knew a wasp or bee flew right behind him in pursuit. As Donald approached, Timmy stood and watched for anything that flew behind Donald so he could swat it away before it stung his young brother.

"Where's it at? Where is it, Timmy?" asked Donald; frightened of the inevitable.

Frantically Timmy looked on and around Donald and waited for a moment. Nothing was there nor flying their way.

"Huh. Well look at that." said Timmy.

"What!? Get it off of me! Hurry!" pleaded Donald as he pulled on his shirt around to see the back of it.

"No… there's nothing on you. It must have been empty." replied Timmy in amazement.

"Shew. Thank goodness." said Donald as a feeling of great relief came over him.

The boys made their way back to the nest which was now lying there in shambles. Still ever so cautious they examined the wreckage.

"What kind of nest is it?" asked Timmy.

"Looks like a hornet's nest."

Timmy squinted his eyes and looked at Donald through the sides "How can you tell?"

Donald looked down at the mangled nest and said, "Dad told me they use their spit, leaves, and grass to make their nests. I think he said they were grey like this too." He leaned down to touch it. "Wow! It looks like they all just died or something."

Through a small opening in the nest Donald saw the remains of many dead insects, he wasn't sure of what type, but he didn't let his brother know any different.

"What happened to them all?" asked Timmy as Donald was carefully tearing the fibers apart to reveal more.

"I don't know. But look at them all!" shouted Donald. He placed his hand under the nest to roll it over when all at once, a sharp pain coursed through his hand. "Ow! Timmy, something stung me!" He rose up holding his hand as tears began to roll down his cheek.

"See, I told you! Get back away from that." said Timmy as he pulled Donald, demanding him to stay away from the nest. "Let me see." Timmy examined the wound.

"It felt like something hit me." cried Donald.

Puzzled by this, Timmy asked, "Hit you?" He further investigated the wound. The stung area was swollen and bleeding; a dark spot already formed around it. "This don't look like a sting from a hornet. What got you, Donald?"

"I don't know." Pain from the sting grew more excruciating.

"Here, hold this on it." said Timmy as he wrapped the bottom of Donald's shirt over the top of his hand. Timmy then began to probe the ground around the nest for any sign of another animal that could have inflicted such damage as that on his brother's hand.

Gradually, he looked around the nest; inching closer and closer until there was nowhere to look but the nest itself. He used his foot to lift the nest and reveal its underside–still nothing. Steadily he pushed the nest all the way onto its other side. No sooner, a small black insect charged from a hole that was concealed by the nest lying on top of it. Timmy let out a shrill of terror as a scorpion attacked and stung his shoe. He stomped the attacker, but with the sound from its crunching exoskeleton; a horde of shiny black and blue scorpions charged from the hole and right up Timmy's leg. Frantically he tried to shake them off, but the strikes from their stingers persisted. His screams could be heard all through the woods.

Moments later Gene tore through the forest to his son's aid. "Timmy! What's wrong?"

"Get them off! Get them off Dad!" screamed Timmy as he frantically swatted scorpions from his arms and legs.

Gene took off his hat and began swiping the scorpions off Timmy's leg. The scorpions were relentless; taking the hit from Gene's hat–getting back up and attacking after Timmy again and again. It did no good; the attackers persisted in their attempts to drain every ounce of venom into Timmy.

"Kill them Daddy!" yelled Donald as he too was being targeted once again. He stomped them as they rushed towards him.

Gene clomped his shoe on the pests. With each thud–a crunch trailed. Seconds later the assault ceased. Just looking at the ground, littered with the mangled bodies of scorpions; Dr. Richards counted at least twenty or more. He knelt down by Timmy and rolled up his pant leg just above the stings from the scorpions. His leg bled from several small holes pierced by the stingers.

"Timmy, how do you feel?" asked Gene as he softly

rubbed the area around a sting.

"It's throbbing, and it stings real bad."

Gene was a little relieved to hear this. He feared Timmy would have no feeling in his leg. "How about you, Donald?"

"It hurts Dad. It's burning." said Donald, wiping the tears that ran down his cheek.

"Alright you two; we've gotta get back to the wagon and head home." Dr. Richards said in a calm voice. "You'll be alright. Will you be okay to walk, Donald?"

"Yeah Dad, I'm fine." replied Donald, who was now a little less worried.

Gene took a handkerchief from his side pocket and wrapped up one of the lesser damaged scorpions and put it in his pocket.

"Keep pressure on your hand, Donald." said Gene as he picked Timmy up in his arms.

Gene packed Timmy and led the way for Donald back out of the woods in a hurry. Once back to their picnic site; Gloria and Margret packed the last of their things into the wagon. Gloria turned to see the boys in their condition and immediately ran to them.

"Oh my goodness, Gene, what happened to them?" asked Gloria.

"Now calm down. We've gotta get back home right now." said Gene with a concerned look, which Gloria recognized right away as a look of worry. She knew he needed her to be calm for the boys.

"Oh my babies." said Gloria as she held a hand to their cheeks.

Dr. Richards examined their stings once again. The tissue around the wounds began to blacken. He knew the scorpions were poisonous and the boys needed help right away.

"What happened to them, Daddy?" asked their

concerned sister Margret as she watched Gene examine them.

He answered, "They got in a mess of scorpions. They're gonna be alright." Quickly he started making his way toward the wagon. "Let's just get on back home."

Gloria picked up Donald and carried him to the wagon. Gene laid Timmy in the back and got his medicine bag. He dug through the old, rugged bag. Its leather had worn over time and been through many trips with Gene to countless people's homes. Once both boys were treated, at least temporarily, Gene, Gloria, and Margret climbed on the front of the wagon.

Gene took the reins and yelled "He-yah!" as he started the horses along their way.

Gene knew that each second counted on the quiet ride home. He kept the horses moving at a quickened pace down the dusty trails that lead to their home. The sun descended close to the mountain tops in the distance. The sky stood as a looming blanket of fiery colors against the calmness of the billowy, purple clouds.

Half an hour later Gene and his family arrived back to their two-story, craftsman-style home. It sat just on the outskirts of Hazel away from all the noise but close enough for patients to have close contact with the doctor. Its whitewashed boards seemed to glow a light purple as the sunset changed everything's appearance. Dr. Richards applied the brake and quickly jumped off the wagon. While Gloria held Donald, she eased down as Margret followed close behind. Gene ran to the back to take Timmy in his arms.

"Let's get them inside." said Gene as he made his way toward their front door.

Once indoors, Gene and Gloria packed the boys to their room. Donald and Timmy were curled into a ball and clutched their arms around each parent's neck. The pain grew stronger with every minute that passed.

"Dad, my legs hurt." said Timmy in a whimpering voice.

"I know Son. Everything will be alright." Gene turned to Gloria, "Stay here with them. I'll go down and get the formula." He turned to go out the door.

"Gene," Gloria's voice cracked.

He stopped and turned to face his wife.

"What if this doesn't work?" whispered Gloria as tears streamed down her face.

"Gloria." Gene stepped over to her and gently placed his hands on her shoulders. He looked deep into Gloria's eyes and said, "This will work. It has to work." Gene turned to exit the room. Gloria placed her clinched fist to her mouth, struggling to keep her composure.

During the past year Gene read in medical journals and newspapers about a man named Albert Calmette of the Pasteur Institute, who created an antivenom for snakes. Gene set out to create an antivenom for scorpion stings. He worked tirelessly and managed to put together a formula that he thought could be a life-saver. Scorpion stings were a very common cause of death in Hazel for children and many adults. The only species known to kill in the area however was the Arizona bark scorpion. The specimen he encountered earlier bared no resemblance to it. Normally, scorpions weren't that aggressive in their attacks on humans and Gene had never heard of a large group of scorpions living and attacking together as the ones in the woods that day.

Dr. Richards made his way back downstairs; through the kitchen and down the hall into his laboratory. A faint ammonia smell filled the small room. Glass beakers and test-tubes were strewn about in an organized mess across two large tables. He rushed over to a shelf that held numerous labeled containers. Gene looked the shelf over for a moment; he found the prepared antivenom sitting on the highest shelf. Gene never actually tested the serum on humans before. After numerous alterations to the formula; including switching from horse blood to rabbit blood, all of his microscope slides seemed to show positive results.

He turned and walked out of the room. On his way back upstairs Dr. Richards second-guessed his formula.

"What if this doesn't work?" he thought. "I could never live with myself knowing I let my sons down. Not only that, let Gloria and Margret down too. They will never trust me again!" His heart raced. "This needs work. Maybe I should try to contact Mr. Calmette himself. Maybe he has something for scorpion stings worked out." He felt the glass beaker slipping in his sweaty hands. A moment passed, "Who am I kidding? That would take far too long. I would be better off letting them lie there to die than do that. I have to try it. There is no other way."

Upon returning to the boys' room, Gene saw their health was fading fast. He rushed over to Timmy's bedside first–he had the most stings and needed quicker attention than his younger brother. Dr. Richards prepared a syringe with the antivenom.

"Now listen Timmy, this may sting a little, but I have to give you and Donald this to make you better. Those scorpions injected venom into you when they stung you." said Gene as he tapped the syringe and pushed the air out of it.

Donald held his covers up to his neck and said, "Daddy, you told me before that poisonous animals made people get sick and die."

Timmy quickly moved his head to Dr. Richards "Dad! Is that true?" he asked.

"Well it used to be. But going by some material that I have studied I've made what's called an antivenom. It fights away the poison."

Gene began to rub a cotton ball, soaked in alcohol, on Donald's arm. "I might have to give you a few more shots to get all of the poison out."

Timmy closed his eyes and squinted tightly as Gene injected the antivenom.

"There you go, buddy. All done." said Gene as he injected the last bit of his formula. A look of relief began to shape Gloria's face as she let out a heavy sigh. "Gloria, would you care to get the boys some water?"

"Sure," said Gloria with a smile.

Gene handed Gloria two small brown packs of opium to add to their water to help ease their pain. He walked over to Donald and started the same procedure he did with Timmy.

"Ouch!" cried Donald as the needle pierced his skin.

"It's alright, Son. It only stings for a second." said Gene, as he tried to comfort Donald.

Gloria made her way back into the room with two glasses of water. She handed Timmy a glass and lovingly rubbed her hand over his hair. She smiled and walked over to Donald's bed. Gene just finished up with Donald.

"Alright, all done." confirmed Dr. Richards.

"Will we have to take another one, Daddy?" asked Donald.

Gene smiled and rubbed Donald's head, "Don't know yet. We'll just have to keep an eye on those stings until they get better."

Gloria gave Donald his glass of water and knelt down to kiss his cheek. "You two will be feeling better before you know it. Me and Daddy will make sure of that."

"Honey, you and Margaret can go ahead to bed if you want. I'll stay up with the boys tonight." said Gene.

"You can't stay up all night. Just whenever you start getting sleepy come and wake me. We'll take turns through the night." suggested Gloria.

Gene took Gloria by her hand. "Alright. These next few hours are crucial, and they need their rest. So you two go ahead, I'll come get you if I start to feel sleepy. There has to be someone here watching them at all times right now, so I don't want to take the chance of falling asleep on them."

"Okay, dear. I love you. Just let me know." Gloria kissed him goodnight and turned to say, "Come on Margret. Let's get some rest. I love you Timmy and Donald. You get some sleep too." As the two walked out of the door and closed it behind them, Gene sat down in a chair in the corner of the room. The two boys were already fast asleep.

Throughout the night Gene kept an eye on their behavior and breathing. He also administered more antivenom to them after timed checks of their wounds. Just a couple of hours before sunrise; Gene began to feel the effects of a long day and a sleepless night wear him down. Gene quietly got up from the chair, opened the door, and eased down the hall into his and Gloria's bedroom. Gene nudged Gloria's arm to wake her.

"Hmm? Is anything wrong?" said Gloria, immediately awake from her light sleep.

"No, everything is fine. I'm getting sleepy is all." replied Gene.

"Ohh. Thank the Lord." Gloria rose up from underneath the covers.

Gene ran his hand through her messy hair. "I had to give them more of the antivenom last night, don't worry, they say it's normal for some to need more than others. I'm gonna need to ride up to Whittlersfield in a few hours after sunrise to get some things, just in case either of the boys happen to have an allergic reaction to the antivenom."

She rubbed her heavy eyes and asked, "How are they now?"

Gene walked to his side of the bed and began to undress. "They're doing good. They've been resting good all night. Just keep an eye on their breathing. If it seems irregular or just anything out of the ordinary come and get me."

Gloria rose up from the bed and pushed the covers away as she slid her legs to the side of the bed. As Gloria's feet touched the cold wooden floor she said, "Alright. Now lay down and get some sleep. You're going to need it if you're making the trip to Whittlersfield in a few hours."

Gene moved the covers back and sat down in the bed. "I love you. Remember, wake me up after sunrise and if you see anything not normal with the boys, come get me." He slid down under the covers.

Gloria finished wrapping the robe around her body as she walked to the door. "Don't worry, I will. Goodnight, get some rest. I love you too."

Gloria closed the door behind her as she left the room. Gene laid there in bed for a moment and thought,

"So far so good."

Chapter 3

"Morning Fred," Deputy Hansen said as he walked into the jailhouse. Fred lay in the cell bed, hat over his eyes. He rose up and rubbed his eyes, trying to get them to focus.

"What time is it?"

Sid rummaged through his desk drawer. "It's about six-thirty in the morning."

Fred tightly closed and opened his eyes. "Jeez. What are you doing in here so early?" said Fred as he then sat up.

Sid pulled a small piece of paper from the drawer and put it in his shirt pocket. "Well I've got some business to tend to on this fine morning."

"Well, well. You seem mighty chipper about this business. What are you gonna do if Percy's left Whittlersfeild by now?"

"I doubt it. If I know anything about Percy, he's not gonna be up this early. And if he is, then he's in no shape to be wandering off to another town." said Sid with a smile on his face.

"Ahh, I see." Fred smiled, "Good thinkin', Deputy."

Sid leaned against the desk facing Fred and crossed his arms. "Yeah, I just hope I know him good enough."

Fred nodded. "I'd say you're right. Now, about getting me outta here?"

"Still working on that one ol' pal." Sid laughed. "Well, I gotta get going. I have to stop by Doctor Richards' place and drop off that medicine he asked me to pick up yesterday."

"Alright. I'll be seein' ya." Fred laid back down and again covered his face with the hat.

Sid grinned, shook his head and walked out of the door.

Several minutes later, Sid drove his wagon towards Dr. Richards' home. The sky shined a brilliant blue with a few billowy clouds floating. It was a warm Sunday morning. Sid smelled the aroma of fried bacon and eggs in the air as he brought the team of horses to a stop. He climbed down from the wagon and approached the front door. He walked up the steps on the porch, and knocked on the door. A few moments passed. The door opened.

"Good morning, Deputy Hansen. Come in." said Margret as she held the door open for the deputy.

Sid removed his hat. "Morning, Margret. How are you doing today?"

Margret tucked in her lips while shaking her head. "Well, not so good. Timmy and Donald are pretty sick right now. I've been worrying about them. But I'm hopeful though."

Sid raised his eyebrows. "Oh, is your daddy around then?"

She nodded. "Yep, hang on and I'll go get him." Margret walked through the living room and down the hallway into the kitchen.

"Come on in, Deputy Hansen," Dr. Richards called from the kitchen.

40

Sid wiped his boots on the wood and proceeded towards the kitchen. Once there his eyes gazed at the smorgasbord of food on the table. Margret sat back down in her place at the table beside of Gloria. Dr. Richards rested at the head of the table.

"Well hello there, come on and have some breakfast with us, Deputy. There's plenty to go around." said Gene.

Gloria held out her hand toward one of the empty chairs. "Yes, you're more than welcome. Please, have a seat." suggested Gloria.

Deputy Hansen stood in the doorway with his hat in hand. "Nah. That's okay folks. Thanks anyways. I've got to be heading on up to Whittlersfield this morning. I was just gonna drop off your supplies I picked up for you yesterday, Doctor."

Gene wiped his mouth and placed the napkin next to his half-eaten plate. "Oh my goodness, I forgot you were supposed to stop by yesterday."

Sid waved at Dr. Richards as he said, "Ah that's alright. No problem."

"I decided to call it a day early yesterday and take the family on a little picnic. Business was slow." He stood from his place at the table and walked toward Deputy Hansen. "I'll help you unload them."

The two walked through the house and out of the front door.

"Yeah, I'm heading up to Whittlersfield myself this morning. I've got a few other things I need to get. Timmy and Donald are a little sick this morning and I need to get some things for them." said Gene as he reached over the side of Sid's wagon to lift one of the wooden crates from the back.

"If you want, you can ride up with me, Doctor. It's a long trip, and I could sure use the company." implied Sid.

"Hey that'd be good. You sure you don't mind?" asked

Gene as his eyes squinted due to the bright sunshine.

"Naw, it's no problem at all." Sid lifted another crate from the back of the wagon.

Gene smiled in gratitude. "Alright then. I'll get this last crate, then get my bag and we'll get along our way."

After unloading the last crate, Gene went inside and grabbed the medical bag. A few minutes later, he and Gloria stepped out onto the front porch. Sid sat on the wagon and waited for Gene. He overhead their conversation.

"We won't be gone long. Like I said before, watch their breathing. I checked their heart rates and they have slowed down quite a bit. I'm starting to worry they might slip into a comma if I don't get them what they need before tonight. Just let them rest for now. You and Margret can go about things around here; they should be fine until I get back."

"Alright, you be careful. I love you." said Gloria as she stood by the front door.

"I love you too." Gene leaned down to give Gloria a kiss. "Margret, help your mommy while I'm gone. I love you."

"I will, Daddy. I love you too." said Margret from inside the house.

Gene walked to Sid's wagon and climbed on.

"Okay, Deputy, let's get on our way." said Gene.

By clicking his cheeks and whipping the reigns, the horses trotted along their way. Gloria and Margret stood on the front porch and waved goodbye. After passing through Gene's white picket fence, Sid guided the team to the right, towards Whittlersfield.

"Thanks for the ride, Deputy. To be honest, I was dreading the long trip alone."

Sid watched the road in front of them. "Hey it's no problem, Doc. I'm not much on the trip myself. It can get pretty boring with no one to talk to."

The two men chatted for a while; discussing the weather, their jobs, and people in town. Sid explained the situation with Percy and Reverend Hopkins' wife to Gene. Gene decided to keep the events that happened the day before with his boy's private for now. He only let Sid believe they were a little sick. For them, the four-hour trip there seemed to pass by quickly.

Back home; the same four hours seemed to drag along slowly for Gloria and Margret. They tried to pass the time by doing chores around the house.

An hour passed since Gloria last checked on Timmy and Donald. She and Margret were in the fenced-in backyard under the warm summer sun, washing clothes in a large metal washtub. Gloria scrubbed the clothes in the soapy water on a washboard. She handed them to Margret to hang on the clothesline to dry.

"It sure is beautiful out today," said Margret and pinned one of Gene's white button-up shirts on the line.

"Yes it is. I just wish Timmy and Donald were able to be out to enjoy it." She rang out another of Gene's shirts.

Margret reached for the shirt and asked, "Do you think Daddy and Deputy Hansen have made it there yet?"

"Hmm." Gloria looked up at the sky and wiped sweat from her brow and took a moment's break. "Yeah. I'd say they've gotten there by now."

"I hope Daddy can help Timmy and Donald get better." said Margret as she too stood there to break for a second. "Has anybody ever lived after they've been stung by scorpions that many times?"

Gloria stayed silent for a moment as she scrubbed a garment. "I'm not sure honey; I know your dad worked very hard to create that antivenom. He's such a good man. All he ever wanted to do since I have known him is help people."

"Yeah. Daddy is a good man." said Margret as she stood there looking down the road that Gene and Sid went that morning. A gentle breeze blew her blonde hair back.

"Honey, would you care to go up and get me some of Timmy and Donald's dirty clothes from their room?" asked Gloria.

"Sure mama." Margret walked into the house, up the stairs and down the hall towards Timmy and Donald's room. Just before opening the door, Margret paused for a second. She let out a heavy sigh and rubbed her tired eyes. Margret stayed awake most of the night with Timmy and Donald on her mind. With a heavy heart filled with sadness and hopefulness, Margret twisted the door knob. She closed her eyes while easing the door open. A light squeak whispered from the hinges. Margret wished so badly for Timmy and Donald to get better. She hated seeing them in the condition they were in the night before.

Slowly she pushed the door, trying not to wake them. With the door opened far enough to see through the crack, Margret was startled to discover both of her brothers up out of their beds. They just stood there; facing the opposite wall and slightly hunched over, as if they were both asleep standing there. Margret opened the door wider to enter the room. She was very confused at how they could stand when mere hours ago they could barely lift an arm. From what she saw, the skin on their arms shown pale-blue, veins clearly visible, looking like tiny, dark spider webs. Margret cautiously entered the room. Confused by what she saw, she quietly said their names.

"Timmy? Donald?"

Her two brothers turned. Their wide eyes were sunk back into their sockets and as red as the nightclothes they wore. Their faces looked just as pale and transparent as the skin on their arms. No sooner than they turned to face her, the two gruesome boys lunged for their oldest sibling. Margret was frightened by their actions, but didn't run. Timmy reached her first. He tackled her with the force of his body slamming into hers. Donald dove to the ground with his arms outstretched. Margret struggled with the two boys for a moment.

She screamed, "What are you doing?" as she struggled with the boys on the floor. Then Margret let out a blood-curdling scream as she felt Timmy's teeth tear through the skin on her upper arm. Donald bit into her shoulder.

Gloria was busy washing clothes outside when she heard Margret's screams coming from inside the boy's bedroom. This instantly sent a bolt of fear through her entire body. Soapy water splashed out of the washtub onto the dry dirt as Gloria dropped the washboard and ran inside. In a panicked-frenzy, she stumbled as she quickly tried to climb the stairs toward Margret's distressed screams. Once to the top, Gloria ran down the hallway to the third door.

Margret heard the pounding of her mother's feet as they met against the dark hardwood of the upstairs floor. The pain was agonizing; she tried everything to break free from the boy's grip. With every second that passed, the boys bit harder and ripped muscles faster, as if the hard bones in Margret's body did nothing but aggravate them.

Gloria darted into the open doorway of the boys' bedroom.

"No!" shrieked Gloria as she cupped both hands over her mouth upon seeing the bloody struggle.

Margret still struggled with her younger brothers; blood loss made her efforts feeble. The glistening of bone showed in places. Blood covered the floor. More was poured from fresh wounds all over the girl.

"Boys! Stop it!" screamed Gloria.

Her terrified cry instantly halted the horrid actions of the boys. Both boys twisted their heads toward Gloria; she stood there trembling, trying desperately to catch her breath. Timmy opened his mouth and let out an unnatural hiss. Part of his tongue was missing a large chunk from the front-left, bitten off during his frenzied chewing and biting. Even though these were her own children, the boys before her were the most appalling sight Gloria ever laid eyes on.

The two moved toward Gloria. With their cold, pale-blue hands outreached, they pounced at her. Survival instinct kicked in, and Gloria realized these were no longer her two loving, rambunctious boys. Instead, they were now more animal than human. Gloria turned to race out of the room and back down the hall. She heard the terrible growling sounds from Timmy and Donald following her out the door; Margret still lay there half-dead. The housedress Gloria wore hindered her ability to run faster. She made it no further than her and Gene's bedroom door just before the stairs. In mid-stride–Donald leaped toward Gloria and wrapped his small arms around her waist. Gloria stumbled and Timmy grabbed her sleeve. The sleeve ripped from the dress as she was drug to the ground. Once there, the boys began to bite into Gloria's arms and neck. She tried to scream for help; it was useless. No one was around for miles. The boys' feast went on for hours.

Chapter 4

Dr. Richards sighed, "Ah, home at last." as he and Deputy Hansen rounded the final curve to his house. Gene was glad to see his home and instantly felt the feeling of longing lift away.

"Yeah, the day has passed by pretty quick." Sid drove the horses onto Gene's property. Once stopped, the two climbed down from the wagon.

"Let me give you a hand with this stuff, Doc." said Sid.

"Hey thanks, Deputy. I'm just gonna run inside real fast and check on Timmy and Donald."

"Okay, that's no problem." Deputy Hansen then uncovered and unloaded one of the many wooden crates from the back of the wagon.

Gene jogged to the front porch and opened the white wooden door leading inside the home. He walked into the living room, looked around, and listened for his family.

Silence.

"Gloria?"

He waited.

"Margret?"

Nothing.

Gene walked toward the hallway; he heard a thud that came from the bottom of the stairway at the end of the hall. It was a sound he heard many times before–someone jumping from the last few steps. He stopped. Gene lowered his brow and listened. He thought to himself, "Now what in the world was that?" The children knew not to jump down the stairs like that. He and Gloria disciplined each of them on separate occasions over it before.

Gene eased around the corner and was stunned. Margret stood there hunched over, peering in the opposite direction into the kitchen. Her long blonde hair was loose and matted to her head by dried blood. His daughter's clothes hung loosely on her body; they, too, bared the same bloody mess as her hair.

"Margret! What happened?" said Dr. Richards as he rushed toward his daughter. His heart pounded inside his chest.

Margret turned her head toward Gene and revealed her half-eaten face and neck. She made a startling noise that sounded as if she gasped for air and screeched all at once. Margret snarled her lips and growled at Gene. Gene's eyes opened wide with fear as he stepped back. Then two more of the same growl-like sounds came from the top of the stairs. Gene looked up; his knees shook as he felt his stomach start to curdle. Timmy and Donald crouched over Gloria's bloody remains and stared straight at Gene with their wide, blood-shot eyes. The boys raised from their mother's body. Her blood covered their hands and faces. All three of the children bore a crazed look, they crept closer to him. Margret charged toward her father with arms grasping. Timmy and Donald clumsily shambled down the stairs. Gene turned to run.

He screamed, "What's happened to you?" All three children chased him through the hall hissing and moaning with each stride. As Gene turned back into the living room, he hit his shoulder against the doorway. Margret seized the opportunity and grabbed the elbow that was thrown behind him by the impact. She sank her teeth through the shirt-sleeve and into warm flesh. Gene let out an excruciating scream. He managed to jerk his arm from Margret's mouth, tearing a large chunk of meat from the back of his arm. Gene let out another painful wail and began running for the open front door.

Gene emerged from the house, grasping his bloody arm and ran straight into Sid.

"What's going on in there?" Sid gasped as he noticed the stream of blood pouring down Gene's elbow onto the porch.

"Get to the wagon, Deputy!" screamed Gene.

Sid didn't have time to ask anything else as the manic children came to the door. He instinctively knew to run— something had gone horribly wrong.

"Something is wrong with them, Deputy!" yelled Sid. "They're not normal!"

"Geez, Doc, I was hoping you'd say that!" yelled Sid, who was terrified and ran behind Dr. Richards.

"They won't stop!" regretfully said Gene as he began to lift himself up into the wagon with his good arm.

Sid drew his pistol from its holster and fired a few shots at their legs. Gene screamed as the bullets tore through his children. The shots made the dreadful trio halt for just a moment. Sid seized the break and jumped into the driver's seat and whipped the horses into a quick gallop. The three children ran close to the wagon at first, straining to get their hands on either man. As they drifted farther from the speeding wagon, Gene could only lay in the back with his head propped up, watching his children chase the wagon and drifting farther away. Each second that passed he grew weaker from the enormous amount of blood loss he suffered. Sid turned to look at the road behind them; the children weren't stopping or even slowing down. They just kept coming. A few moments later they were only specks in the distance.

Sid glanced between the road before them and the vanishing children. "Doctor Richards, what just happened back there?"

Gene sat in a daze. His head bobbed around with the bumps in the road as he stared back in the direction of his children. He weakly replied, "I messed it up."

Chapter 5

Fred took a break from reading and mumbled, "What's a guy gotta do to get some food around here?" Eating was on his mind after going almost an entire day without so much as a bite. He got up from the cot and walked to the cell's bars. As he peered through the window on the other side of the jailhouse, he noticed what a busy day it was in town. The sun shone bright and everyone seemed to be out enjoying the Sunday afternoon.

Fred put his arms through the bars and leaned his forehead against them.

"You've really done it this time, Fred," he said. He took in a deep breath and sighed. Softly, Fred hit his fists against the bars and turned to lie back on the bed and continue reading.

After adjusting his pillow for comfort, there came a huge uproar just outside of the jailhouse. Fred paid the disturbance no attention at first, thinking it was just a fight or just some drunks causing trouble outside. Without warning, the door to the jailhouse burst open. In came Sid helping Gene to an empty cell beside of Fred's.

Fred asked, "What happened to you, Doctor?" He stood and went to the front of his cell once again.

Sid carefully tried to ease Dr. Richards down. "He was attacked just a few minutes ago."

"By what?" Fred asked; amazed by the wound he saw on the doctor's arm.

"Hang on Fred, I need to go get some stuff." Sid ran outside to his wagon. Half of the medical supplies that were supposed to be dropped off at Gene's were still in it.

Once outside, Sid ran to the back of the wagon and found one of the crates. He grabbed it and hurried in the jailhouse. He placed the crate on the floor, lifted the lid and rummaged through its contents. He found some bandages, new beakers and test tubes in the wooden box. Quickly, he grabbed the bandages and laid them to the side and ran outside once again to do the same with another crate.

Just as with the last crate, Sid laid it on the jailhouse floor and lifted the lid. This one held some antiseptic inside, which he gathered and brought over to Gene's bed, along with the bandages.

"Alright Doctor Richards, we're gonna get you fixed up now, okay?" said Deputy Hansen.

"Alright, pour slow." said Gene. He could barely speak through the pain.

Sid poured the antiseptic on the wound. Gene screamed in agony as the burning sensation only intensified the pain in his arm.

"Alright. Now let me help you get it bandaged up," said Sid as he unrolled some of the white cloth bandage. Carefully, he wrapped it around Gene's arm, making sure it was very snug around the wound to staunch the bleeding.

"So what happened out there, guys?" asked Fred once again.

Sid tied the end of the bandage into a knot. "Something is wrong with Doctor Richards' kids."

Fred asked, "Are they hurt too?"

"To tell you the truth, I'm not too sure what's going on myself," Deputy Hansen pointed out. He pushed the cork back into the bottle of antiseptic. "What really is going on Doctor Richards?"

"I really don't know." replied Gene. He was very weak and barely held his head up. "It all started yesterday evening when both of the boys were stung by a whole mess of scorpions."

"That's not good," Fred said.

Gene continued, "The scorpions were like none I've ever seen before. Have you heard of something called antivenom?"

"Nope." answered Fred.

Gene coughed. "Well, it's supposed to counteract the venom in animal bites, in this case–scorpion stings. A doctor has made one to stop the effects of snake venom. Well, I tried my hand at making one for scorpion stings. I never tested it on humans until now."

Fred's eyes grew wide as he looked around the room. "Doc! Are you serious? You used it on your kids without knowing if it was going to work or not?" asked Fred.

"Yes! I know I never should have done that," screamed Gene as tears poured down his face. "I knew better. What have I done to them? My life is over!"

Sid said, "Doctor. Richards–"

"I'm not a doctor! Don't call me one! Doctors cure people, not turn them into maniacs!"

Sid grabbed Gene by his shoulders. "Stop it! You didn't do anything wrong! You were trying to help your family! That's something any man would've done." stated Deputy Hansen. "You don't know that's what got into those kids. What kind of medicine could ever make somebody act the way they did?"

Dr. Richards moved his head back and forth on the pillow. "I don't know. Maybe it was something with the mixture and the venom. It might have done something to their minds." he suggested.

Sid swallowed the knot in his throat as he asked, "If I may, where was Gloria when you went inside?"

Gene's mouth stretched into a huge frown as he tried to hold back tears. "She was dead. Her body was lying at the top of the stairs. Timmy and Donald were over top of her. They were eating."

Fred shifted. "Do what? You mean those kids done that to your arm?"

"Yes, one of them bit me while chasing me out of the house."

"And you think they were trying to–" Fred stopped for a moment as he realized what he was about to say. "Eat you?"

Sid stepped out of the cell and over to Fred's. "You don't understand. I was there. You should have seen the look of those kids. They just had such a terrible demeanor. It was like they were hunting us, kinda like animals or something."

Fred held his head back and rubbed his eyes with his thumb and finger as he said, "This is just getting too weird!"

Sid walked back over to the cell Gene was in. He noticed the doctor trying to sit up, but fading in and out of consciousness.

"Just lay down, Doc. You need to rest," said Deputy Hansen as he helped Gene stretch out in the bed. As soon as his head hit the pillow, Gene was fast asleep. Sid got up and walked out of the cell, leaving the door open just in case he needed to get to Dr. Richards quickly again.

Fred stood at the front of his cell with his hands

tightly grasping the bars.

"What's going on here, Sid? You swear all of that happened?" inquired Fred.

Sid looked straight into Fred's eyes and said, "Yeah, Fred. I swear every bit of that happened. It's no lie." He broke his stare and leaned against the wall next to Fred's cell. "I just don't know what could've gotten into them kids to make them to do something so horrible."

Fred watched Sid's face flush with frustration. "Do you think the doctor could be right? Could that stuff he gave them really cause their minds to warp like that?"

Deputy Hansen rubbed his forehead. "I don't know. It's hard to imagine that being the cause; but really, though, it's hard to imagine them actually trying to eat somebody too. So I guess it's possible."

Fred's lip twitched. "According to the doctor, they didn't just try to eat somebody, they ate their own mother!" He took a breath. "Did you go in the house with him?"

Sid shook his head as he looked around the room. "No, I was outside unloading some of the supplies he brought back from Whittlersfield. When I stopped by this morning everything seemed to be fine. He just mentioned the boys were sick and that he was heading to Whittlersfield to get more supplies. I offered him a ride with me since I was going myself." Sid paused; chills ran down his spine as he remembered the first sight of the kids running to the door after Dr. Richards. "We got back and he was in a hurry to go check on the boys. I figured I'd stay outside and start unloading the stuff for him. He couldn't have been inside for just a minute when I heard him just let out the most awful scream I have ever heard. Then they came running out of the house. He was holding his arm and the kids were making these hissing sounds." Sid looked at the ground and shook his head.

"All three of them were covered with blood. We barely got away." He looked back up to the ceiling as he took in a deep breath. "I tried to shoot them in the legs to stop them, but it didn't do any good! They just kept running after us. Even after we got a good distance from them, you could see them running. Well, not really running. More like limping really fast. I just kept driving till we didn't see them anymore."

"Man," Fred said with a disgusted look.

"Yeah. Exactly." said Sid. He walked over to his desk and sat in the chair. He laid his head down on the cool wood. Fred too went to sit down on the cot in his cell, trying to take in everything he just heard.

Half an hour passed by while Sid slipped off to sleep with his head still lying on the desk. Dr. Richards slept as well. Fred stayed awake. He was still bothered by everything Sid said. Fred glanced out of the window for a moment as a man ran towards the jailhouse. The man's attention was drawn away by someone outside. He pointed toward the jailhouse and resumed his dash.

"Hey, Sid! You'd better wake up. I think there's some guy heading this way."

Sid quickly raised his head and turned to look out the window. The man ran straight to the door and burst inside.

"Where's the sheriff at?" the man asked.

Deputy Hansen sat up in his chair as he grasped the arm rests. "Don't know, he should be somewhere around town. Why, what's going on?" He recognized the man as Harold Sanderson from the mill.

Harold looked very concerned about something. He replied, "You need to come with me, Deputy!"

Sid got up, and looked at Fred with great concern. He asked Harold again, "What's happening?"

Harold was visibly upset. "You ain't gonna believe

me, Deputy. You just need to come on!"

Sid walked quickly to the door. Harold began running, and so did Sid after shutting the door.

Sid caught up to Harold and asked, "What's going on, Harold?"

"There's some kids covered in blood that came into town and just started attacking people!"

"When did they get here?"

Harold, tired and out of breath, said, "Just a–few minutes ago. They just came running in here and–started tearing through the place, jumping on people and–biting them!"

Sid already knew the answer to the question he was about to ask, "How many of them were there?"

"Three of 'em." Harold led Sid to the scene.

The sound of a commotion grew louder as the two men came closer to Hazel's thick wooden gates. The tall gate was the only way in and out; the rest of the town was surrounded by a large canyon wall. The town sprang up long ago from pueblo ruins, the leftovers of an old fort.

People were screaming and ran past the men in the opposite direction, desperate to escape the riot that had broken out.

Sid exclaimed, "Dear Lord!" Everyone was in a frenzy. Many people ran around; some were lying in pools of their own blood. Deputy Hansen glanced around, looking for Dr. Richards' children.

"Over there's one of 'em!" said Harold pointing toward a huddle of men that restrained Timmy.

"C'mon!" said Sid as he ran to aid the men.

Sid and Harold had to be careful where they stepped because so many wounded people were lying on the ground. Some bore only a few gashes on their bodies and were getting to get to their feet. Others had life-threatening wounds and were lying motionless.

As they neared Timmy, both men saw Margret chasing a woman who carried a baby.

"Margret!" screamed Sid as he and Harold quickly stopped and changed directions. She was reaching out to grab the back of the woman's dress. Harold drew his pistol and fired a shot at Margret's legs. His shot hit its mark and Margret fell to the ground. The woman she chased continued running. Harold ran toward Margret, seizing the opportunity to pin her down.

"Wait, Harold!" yelled Sid. Harold ignored the deputy and jumped on top of Margret as she got to her knees. He pushed her blood-covered face to the ground and tried to hold her arm behind her back. Margret squirmed uncontrollably and managed to turn her body so that she was lying on her back. Everything happened so fast, Sid didn't have time to react. A split-second later, Margret stretched her neck enough to bite a large chunk of meat from Harold's hand. Blood gushed out and poured down his arm. Harold screamed in agony and quickly fell to his back. Margret immediately pounced on Harold.

"No!" yelled Sid.

Harold tried to hold Margret's head back with his good hand. "Get her off me!"

Deputy Hansen opened fire on Margret. Blood sprayed from the entry wounds with each hit he made. Margret's body jerked as she sank her teeth into Harold's neck. He let out yet another painful scream. Blood gushed into his esophagus; his screams became muffled and quickly changed into gurgling sounds as his airway flooded with blood.

Sid stumbled backwards. He felt like he was about to faint as his knees began to buckle. Everywhere around him utter chaos reigned. He saw all three of Dr. Richards' children. Each of them attacked innocent people.

They couldn't be stopped.

Nothing worked, not even gunshots and Sid was beginning to realize that.

He watched helplessly and thought, "How can this be possible? It's like they've got special powers or something!" His heart pounded and his breath grew short. He felt panic rise.

The situation had gotten out of control and there was nothing he could do. Sid hesitantly turned around. His feet were heavy as he started to run. Nothing seemed real anymore and everything seemed to happen in slow-motion.

Chapter 6

"Ohh! He–help! Somebody help me! Please," moaned Dr. Richards.

Fred stood up and walked to his cell door. "Hey Doc. Just hold on a few minutes, somebody will be here to get you what you need." He tried to keep Gene calm.

"I need help! Come over here!" pleaded Dr. Richards.

"I can't right now, Doc! I'm locked up in the next cell. Deputy Hansen will be back in just a minute. Just hold on till he gets here."

"No! I need somebody now!" demanded Gene. "Help me please."

Frustrated, Fred sighed. "I can't. Just hold on he'll be back soon." A moment passed as silence settled back in.

"Who's that?" asked Gene. His voice, filled with worry and confusion.

"Who are you talking about?" Fred looked around the jailhouse and out of the window to see who Gene was talking about.

"Who are you?"

Fred stood silent for a moment as he tried to figure out what was going on with Gene. "It's me Doc, Fred

Douglas." Silence filled the jailhouse. "You hear me, Doc?"

Still no response.

"Doctor. Richards, hang in there. Help is on the way." Silence filled the room once again. Fred heard Gene breathing slowly, and assumed he'd fallen back asleep.

Everything seemed to be okay, Fred turned around and lay back down on his bed.

Gene let out a deafening scream.

"Doctor. Richards! What's wrong?" Fred feared the worst. He ran to the wall facing the outside and yelled, "Hey! Can anybody hear me out there? Somebody! We need help in here!"

Gene continued to scream as his body convulsed for a few more seconds.

The screaming stopped abruptly.

Fred walked back to the cell door to listen once again. He stood there with his hands clinched around the cold iron bars.

Silence.

All Fred heard was his pounding heart.

"Doc?"

Silence reigned.

Fred bowed his head and stared at the dirty floor. With a heavy sigh he said, "I'm sorry, Doc."

Minutes passed by and Fred stood with his head bowed in silent reverence. He heard voices yelling outside. They were too muffled to clearly comprehend any words. The voices grew louder. Soon the people were close enough so that Fred recognized one of them. Deputy Hansen told people to follow him into the jailhouse.

The steel-reinforced door quickly swung open. Sid hurried everyone inside.

Sid yelled, "Hurry! Get in!" A small cluster of people flocked inside. Each of them bore expressions of horror.

When the last one entered, Sid slammed the door shut and slid the metal blockade in place. In total, there were ten people that followed the deputy inside.

Fred recognized everyone. There was Mr. Rusty Martin and his wife, Bella, who were an older couple and lifetime residents of the town. Widow Octavia Helmsley and her daughter Susan. Steven Jones, the local blacksmith. Ronald Smith, Dave Wither, and Felix Carter; all three worked in the coal mine. Ronald was with his wife Silvia and son Michael.

Husbands held their families in open arms. Both children cried. Octavia knelt and tried desperately to calm her daughter.

"Is everyone alright?" asked Sid as he tried to gather himself.

"Yeah. What's gotten into those kids?" asked Steven Jones trying to catch his breath as well.

Bella Martin yelled, "It's the devil!" She raised her head from her husband's chest. Tears flowed fresh down her wrinkled face.

Rusty had his arms around her and petted her head. "They were eating those people, I tell you!"

Everyone yelled over each other to Sid about what they just saw. Deputy Hansen glanced over at Fred, who stood at the cell door. Fred motioned him to look over at Gene. Distracted by everyone's chattering, the deputy glanced back and forth at the people around him and Gene's lifeless body.

"Everybody just calm down!" yelled Sid. A hush fell over the group. He walked over to Gene. The doctor's body was sprawled out with his left arm and leg draped off of the bed. Sid approached the cell door. Everyone watched as he slowly opened the door completely.

"That's Doctor Richards!" said Octavia. Dr. Richards spent many sleepless nights by her husband's bedside, caring for him just before he died.

Sid placed his hand on Gene's chest. He looked at the expression on the good doctor's face as he felt for a heartbeat. Gene's eyes were wide open and so was his mouth. Sid couldn't feel a heartbeat, so he carefully placed Gene's arm and leg back on the bed. He shut the doctor's eyes with his hand and placed the raggedy quilt over his head. Sid stood there for a moment trying to gather himself.

Octavia watched Deputy Hansen along with all the others. "Is he dead?" she asked.

Sid looked at her and nodded.

"Those were his kids out there!" yelled Felix Carter. His large biceps bulged and his black skin glistened with sweat as he pointed at the doctor's body. "Wasn't it, Deputy? They were his!" Felix's size made him seem quite intimidating at first sight.

Sid nodded. "Yes it was."

"Then what's going on here, Deputy?" asked Ronald Smith. He stepped forward from the back of the group. Sweat beaded on his tanned skin as well. He too was a very muscular man.

"Did they kill him too?" asked Octavia. Everyone began asking questions and the room once again filled with incomprehensible chatter.

"Hey! Calm down everybody!" yelled Sid with his hands held out. No one stopped. "Listen!"

Everyone fell silent.

Sid explained, "I don't know what happened to the kids. All I know is me and Doctor Richards went to Whittlersfield this morning. He mentioned his boys were sick and needed to get medicine. His little girl greeted me at the door this morning when I showed up, she seemed fine." He stopped to wipe the sweat away from his mouth. "Now when we got back he went in to check on his boys and the next thing I know, he comes running out the door with blood pouring out of his arm and those little monsters chasing him outta there." He looked around the room. "I tried to shoot them, but it didn't do any good, just like out there. We got in the wagon and got outta there. They chased us up the road, then we lost sight of 'em. He told me and Fred earlier the boys were scorpion stung and he tried out a new medicine on them. He thought maybe something in the medicine changed with the venom from the stings and caused the kids to flip their noodle. That's all I know."

Nobody said a word. They just stood there in disbelief.

"Didn't the guy even know what that stuff would do to them?" asked Felix.

Deputy Hansen's eyes locked with Felix's. "I don't know what he was thinking. I guess he just panicked and felt like he didn't have nowhere else to turn."

"We're gonna have to figure out what to do. People are dying out there and we need to figure something out quick!" said Ronald Smith.

"You're right, Ronald. We need to go out and get as many people in here as we can. It's probably the safest place in town." Sid walked to the back room. When he returned he had enough guns for the men. "Here boys. Ladies, y'all stay here and if anybody comes knocking to get in, let them in."

Just as Sid finished talking there was a loud pounding at the door. The deputy quickly ran to the door, slid the blockade and opened the door.

"What is going on around here, Deputy?" It was Sheriff Wellman. His clothes were dirty and his face dripped sweat.

Sid was anxious to get out of the door. "I'll explain later, Sheriff. We've gotta get as many people in here as we can." The deputy stepped toward the door but Sheriff

Wellman moved in front of him.

"I want answers and nobody's going nowhere till I get 'em!"

From the door of his cell, Fred said, "It seems like there's some people out there that's actually hungrier than you, Sheriff."

"Hey! Let me tell you something, funny man," said Sheriff Wellman. He walked quickly toward Fred as he reached into his coat, pulled out a pistol and pointed it straight at Fred. "I've got half-a-mind right now to blow your face off!"

Everyone in the room gasped. Fred stood there with a smirk on his face as he chuckled.

Sid yelled, "Sheriff!" Wellman turned his head to the deputy. "We ain't got time for your stupid games. There's bigger fish to fry right about now in case you didn't notice!"

Sheriff Wellman was dumbfounded. Sid never talked to him like that. The sheriff lowered his gun and turned to face everyone.

"Now, you gonna join us and put them bullets to some good use or what?" asked Sid. Tolerance for Sheriff Wellman dwindled since his stealing and murdering ways came to light.

Sheriff Wellman squinted his eyes as he looked at Sid. Anger boiled up inside as he said, "No Deputy. You go on."

"Alright, have it your way, Sheriff. C'mon, men." All of the men followed him out of the door. Octavia held her daughter, Susan close. Bella crossed her arms and turned away from the confrontation as Sylvia held her son's shoulders in front of her.

Sheriff Wellman walked towards the back room and said, "Instead of just standing there being useless, why don't one of you women lock that door. I don't want none of those maniac kids getting in here."

Offended, the women all looked around at each other. Ronald Smith's wife, Silvia, walked over and slid the blockade back in place. No sooner than she did this, there came a loud pounding on the door. She quickly slid it back and pulled the door open. It was Rusty Martin. He stumbled inside and sat in the nearest chair. Silvia shut the door and put the blockade back in place.

"What's wrong, Honey?" asked his wife, Bella as she came to his side. Rusty looked up at her. Everyone saw the fear in his eyes.

"They're walking out there," Rusty said as he struggled to catch his breath.

Bella shook her head as she tried to understand what he meant. "Who is? What are you talking about, Rusty?" she asked.

"The people," He looked around the room and could hardly speak. "We saw them die! It can't be!"

Octavia walked over and knelt down beside of him and asked, "Rusty, we don't know what you mean. What are you saying?"

He shook his head as he paled. "The dead people. They're walking around now."

Sylvia's mouth dropped as she looked to Octavia. Octavia's eyes were wide as she glanced at the others.

Bella looked up at the other women and back to her husband. She held his hand even tighter as she asked, "Rusty, are you sure it was the same people?"

"Yes! They started chasing Deputy Hansen and the others as soon as we stepped out there!" He stared straight ahead. "Every one of them took off running!"

Octavia stood up and walked over to the window to look out.

"Dear Lord! It's true!"

Chapter 7

"Where did they all come from?" yelled Sid as he and the other men ran through the streets.

Felix looked behind him to check one more time. "Those guys were dead earlier!" screamed Felix. The men ran down an alley way trying to outrun the horde of ghouls behind them. Dave Wither turned around and fired two shots at their pursuers.

"They won't die!"

"Buddy, I don't know if you were listening or not, but those people already died!" replied Felix.

"Ain't no way!" commented Dave as they ran out the other side of the alley.

Sid ran toward Randal's Mercantile. "Guys, in here!" The four men raced inside. Once everyone entered the building the deputy slammed the door shut.

"Get something to block this door!" said Steven Jones as he frantically looked around the store. As Sid and Steven pushed against the door with all of their body weight, Felix, Ronald, and Dave scoured the store for anything heavy enough to hold the door shut.

Ronald found a heavy wooden display table near

the counter. "Come help me!" demanded Ronald. The two men ran to help Ronald. Numerous pieces of fine porcelain figurines and glassware covered its rugged surface. Felix and Dave shoved everything off of the display. The valuable goods shattered as they hit the wooden floor. The three men then lifted the table and started moving it to the door. The glass and porcelain debris crunched under their heavy feet as they tried to hurry before the monsters broke through the door.

"Watch out." Ronald said as the men came close to the door. Sid and Steven quickly moved away from the door.

Once the hefty table was in place, Deputy Hansen pulled his hat off and wiped the sweat from his brow as he said, "Alright, that should hold 'em for now." He placed his hat back on his head and continued. "And you say those people were dead earlier?"

Felix held his hands on his hips and looked up at the ceiling, trying to rest. "Yeah. Every one of 'em."

Sid scratched his head as he looked around the room. He tried to process everything that had happened up to that point–no matter how unbelievable. Nothing was too far-fetched to overlook anymore. He thought out loud. "Maybe it's some kind of sickness."

Steven, who was visibly unnerved by all of the events said, "It's sick, alright!"

Dave stood by the counter with his arms folded. "It could be, Deputy. Cause those people out there right now got bit by those kids." he said.

Sid was trying hard to believe everything. "Do you guys know for sure if they were actually dead or not?" he asked.

"Can't be real sure, Deputy, but usually when somebody's injured that bad they don't live very long." said Ronald as he looked around at the other men.

Sid rubbed the back of his sweaty neck. "That's true, but it would just make a lot more sense to me if they were laying there alive." he admitted.

"There ain't nothing making much sense right now, Deputy. Dead or alive, it don't much matter. They're still eating people." said Felix. He looked over Sid's shoulder and noticed the table inching away from the door. The corpses outside were shoving the door, trying to make their way inside. "And if we don't get out of here, we're next on the menu."

"That's great." said Sid as he looked for a way out.

Steven ran to the back of the store and yelled, "Over here! We can get out back this way." The others followed as the table scooted further from the door. As the group gathered at the back door, Sid began explaining what they needed to do next.

"Alright boys, we've all agreed that this is some kind of sickness, right?"

Ronald nodded. "That's the best thing we can figure right now."

"We need to get out of town and try to make it to Whittlersfield to get help. Maybe we can get enough people to come back to Hazel. Hopefully with enough of us, we'll be able to do something about all of this." explained Sid.

Ronald shook his head and asked, "What about everyone back at the jailhouse?"

Sid nodded. "They'll all be safe where they are. There ain't no way anything will be able to get inside of that place. It's a lot safer in there than running around out here."

Ronald nervously rubbed the side of his unshaved face. "I don't know, Deputy. Whittlersfield is an awful long way."

"I know, but it's the closest town. We have to do

something, Ronald or else we're all gonna wind up just like them people out there." Sid stepped up to Ronald, placed his hand on his shoulder and looked him in the eyes. "I promise your family is gonna be okay. I understand you're worried, but we gotta do this for us all."

Ronald stood silent for a moment looking at the floor of the mercantile. He began nodding his head in approval. "Alright, let's go."

Sid patted Ronald on his back and asked, "Anybody else got any questions? I know it's a long trip, but it's our only choice."

Dave looked back at the front door. "They're about to get in here! We need to move!" Everyone else looked; the corpses outside nearly had the table pushed completely away from the door. Many of them had their arms and hands reaching inside. A few ghouls had their faces pressed against the crack between the door, chomping their teeth. The dead groaned and grunted as they used their sheer strength in numbers to push the sturdy wooden door.

"Go. Now!" screamed Sid.

Felix quickly twisted the door handle and swung the door open. To everyone's surprise there weren't any of the dead outside the door. As each of them exited the store, they jumped down the three steps that lead up to the door. Steven was the last to the doorway. He heard the table turn over and hit the wooden floor as the dead forced their way into the mercantile. The ghouls flooded into the store. Steven fumbled for the door handle, trying to grab it to shut the door. A couple of ghouls inside the store saw him standing in the back doorway and shuffled toward him. At last, his shaking hand grasped the knob. Hungry hordes raced toward him, knocking over porcelain dishes and fancy glasses. Steven's eyes grew wide as he watched them move toward him–he slammed the door shut and jumped down the steps.

Sid clapped a hand on Steven's back as he joined the rest of them. "Let's get to the gate. Everybody watch and don't let none of them sneak up on us."

Felix said, "Alright, let's do this!"

The group moved toward the town's entrance. Sid carefully checked each street and alley they traveled. The others followed Sid's lead. Each of them watched with alert eyes. Timidly, they made their way through the street; running for brief moments, then hiding behind buildings as they looked for the safest route. Their footsteps were light, and their guns were ready. Each man cautiously looked down every street and behind every building for any sign of movement. Silence filled the town; everything seemed too calm.

With the gate in sight just ahead on the right, the men gathered at the end of an alley, between the post office and hotel.

Deputy Hansen grinned and whispered, "There it is boys. We're almost out of here."

"If we can find some horses along the way, we can make it there and back a lot quicker." said Ronald.

Sid went over the plan with the men one more time, "Alright, now remember, keep your eyes around us at all times. It's hard tellin' where any of these people might be along our way. If we stick close together and watch, we should be okay." He looked around at all of the men. Each of them seemed to have a glimmer of hope in their eyes. "Now let's take it steady like we have been." He leaned to the corner of the hotel to peak out of the alley and make sure everything was clear. Nothing was in sight except the large wooden gates standing there wide open as they normally did. He leaned back and turned to the men again to say, "Let's go."

As the group eased out of the alley, Sid stopped

abruptly in front of the group. He pointed across the street. A disheveled man limped in the opposite direction of them. He wore a light-blue shirt, stained with blood on the back.

Felix leaned over to Sid while continuing to watch the lurking man. "Ain't that Tyler Brum?" he whispered.

Sid nodded. "Yeah, I think so."

"Is he one of them?"

"I'm not sure."

Ronald nudged Sid anxiously. "It don't matter. Let's just keep quiet and get out of here."

Sid held a concentrated stare on Tyler as he wandered around. "Alright, let's move. Let's just keep an eye on him." he softly said.

Ronald nodded; the group carefully walked toward the entrance. The gates were made of heavy, solid logs and were open to the inside. The canyon's sheer cliff walls that surround Hazel came around to this opening where the gate was built to completely close off the town if it was ever needed.

They approached one of the large gate doors and eased to the edge of it. Sid glanced at Tyler, who continued to walk in the opposite direction. The others watched for the signal from the deputy to move. Once Sid felt convinced Tyler was not concerned with them, he motioned his head toward the entrance. The men jogged through the gates and came to an abrupt stop just outside. A group of fifteen dead people staggered around on the outside of the entrance. They immediately noticed Sid and the others.

The deputy's eyes grew wide as his heart dropped into his stomach. He and the rest of the men stepped back as all of the dead turned toward them. Sid drew his pistol and fired. The others followed suit and fired their weapons at the ghouls. The well placed shots tore through each of the monsters. Blood sprayed from each bullet hole as they hit the bodies. The unstoppable horde moved toward them.

"Get back in and shut the gate!" Sid ordered.

They dropped back. Felix and Dave went to the left door. They wedged themselves between the door and rocky wall, then slowly pushed the door closed. Sid and Ronald did the same on the right. Both men struggled as they barely moved the doors. Veins bulged with effort.

Steven stood in the entrance blasting his shotgun as the dead rushed toward them. The men fought with all of their might and still only moved the doors inches. As Dave and Felix struggled with the door, Dave noticed Tyler creeping slowly down the street, he watched as Tyler came to a stop.

"What's he doing?"

"Who?" asked Felix.

"Tyler."

Felix looked as Tyler stood there for a moment. His head tipped back and appeared to scan the sky for something.

Both doors were nearly halfway closed.

Tyler managed three steps and turned his side to the men. His lips were gone and his teeth were stained red. Dave gasped as Tyler revealed his gruesome appearance.

"He's a biter all right!" said Felix as he pushed even harder to close the door.

Steven's shots helped slow down the approaching ghouls. Each shot resulted in a brief pause in their steps. After another shot, Steven put the shotgun down from his cheek and opened the bullet chamber. He reached his hand down in the leather bag that hung from his shoulder to grab more shells.

"I'm out." he muttered as he brushed the stitches in the bottom of the small bag with his fingertips.

The gate was now more than a third of the way closed.

Steven ran over with Sid to assist him and Ronald. Half a moment passed and their side was shut. They ran to help Felix and Dave.

With small steps, Tyler turned towards their direction.

The gate was finally closed, Ronald ran by the large wooden blockade and pushed it through the hole on the other side of the gate to lock it. Sid hurried to turn around to see where Tyler was. As soon as he turned, his eyes met with Tyler's hungry, red eyes; he stared directly at Sid and the others.

"Great." said Sid. "Run, boys. Run!" He fired a shot at Tyler as he and the others turned to run for the jailhouse. Tyler moaned, held both hands out, and started for them. Everyone ran back down the alley between the post office and hotel. Once through the alley they all stopped to check if the way was clear. To their left was a small group of eight corpses.

Ronald pointed to the right and said, "Everybody, this way!"

As soon as they resumed running, Tyler stumbled his way into the alley in pursuit. Tyler stopped on the other side. He let out a hiss and continued the search. This attracted the attention of the ghouls walking around to the left of the alley; they too began pursuing the men.

Felix looked behind them as they turned the corner near the mill. He saw the hungry mob shambling full-force behind them. "We've got more biters a comin'."

"We're not far now. Just keep running!" yelled Deputy Hansen and flagged the men onward across the bridge over the small stream that powered the mill's water wheel.

The screams of a man and woman echoed through the streets. They weren't far from the group.

The men ran past the mercantile where they were first held up. The back door now barely hung by one of its hinges outside.

"Those things ain't in there anymore." said Felix as they turned another corner around the store.

Ronald came to an unexpected stop. "That's cause they're all out here!"

The street in front of them was filled with the dead. A few of them huddled around freshly killed victims and others walked around mindlessly. Nearly thirty of them staggered about from one end of the street to the other.

The group that already chased them let loose moans everyone heard just around the corner behind them.

Steven stumbled backwards. "They're everywhere!" His face grew pale as he hyperventilated. Consumed with fear, he looked for somewhere to run. Suddenly he bolted inside the mercantile. Ronald tried to stop him.

"Steven! No!"

It was too late. Steven's screams filled the air as a biter inside the store grabbed him. His screams drew the attention of many of the dead out in the street.

"No," grunted Sid. He took in the scene before them. The biters that had been idly shambling around now made their way toward them.

"This ain't good," Felix said as he saw the first group of infected make their way around the mercantile's corner.

Each man fired their guns at the biters.

Realizing the uselessness of their actions, Sid yelled, "This ain't gonna work! We've gotta get out of here!" He saw old man Hawkins' house with its front door wide open. Through the house he could see the backdoor standing open as well. "Everybody in here!"

The group followed the deputy into the house. Inside, they ran past a man and woman biter that were hunched over a human corpse, tearing it apart and devouring the entrails. After the men ran by, the two rose to their feet and joined the chase.

As the men reached the door in the back of the house

Sid yelled to Felix, who was in the back of the group, "Shut the door on your way out!"

"Of course! That's only common courtesy, Deputy!"

Every biter from the street flooded inside the home. The men all passed through the door. Felix stopped for a second to slam the door shut behind him. He grabbed the door and swung it. One of their pursuers was too close; the door hit the biter, and it fell to the ground.

"That didn't work." said Felix as he turned to join the other men on the street behind the house. The mob began pouring out of the house, trampling the ghoul struck by the door.

The men once again took to their heels. Sid yelled, "Let's go! The jailhouse isn't much further!"

"You said that last time, Deputy!" commented Felix.

"Well let's hope we don't run into any more trouble."

Felix looked back at the horde behind him. "Well trouble is still following us! So we need to get there soon."

The men continued running down the street, taking the long way back to the jailhouse.

Chapter 8

Everyone quietly sat in the jailhouse awaiting the return of Deputy Hansen and the others. Rusty Martin lay on the floor with a blanket covering him as his wife, Bella sat nearby, keeping a check on his condition. Ronald's wife Silvia paced the jailhouse floor while occasionally checking out the window.

"I hope they're alright."

Her son Michael sat in the corner, arms wrapped around knees. He looked up as his mother glanced out the window once again. "Momma? Daddy's gonna come back for us, ain't he?" She knelt down beside of him, gently took his chin and said, "Of course he is, child." She smiled and rubbed his head. "Your daddy's gonna fight and do everything he can to get to us."

Just then Sheriff Wellman shouted from the back room. "No he ain't, boy! You're daddy's a goner just like those other idiots that went with him!"

Everyone was appalled by what the sheriff said and looked toward the back room.

"Sheriff!" gasped Silvia.

"Sheriff, sheriff!" replied Sheriff Wellman in a high pitched voice, mocking Silvia. "I ain't lying!"

Everyone heard Wellman's shoes scuff across the floor. He stumbled out of the room and leaned against the wall.

"You all are gonna die!" muttered Sheriff Wellman. The children in the room began crying. Everyone else traded concerned glances. Sylvia stared at Wellman as she shook her head. No one could believe the way Sheriff Wellman was behaving.

"Sheriff! Stop it right now! You're scaring everyone!" demanded Silvia.

The sheriff gave Silvia an enraged look and stumbled toward her. "Hey! Let me tell you something!" He pointed his fingertip at his chest. "I'm the sheriff around here and there ain't gonna be nobody... and I mean nobody gonna tell me what to do. Especially a woman!"

Silvia stood strong as Sheriff Wellman came toward her. Fred, who was reading Sid's Bible, put it down and walked to his cell door. Sheriff Wellman walked up to Silvia and stood just inches from her. He squinted his eyes and leaned in close.

He quietly said, "You trying to undermine my authority woman?"

Silvia cringed in disgust as the heavy stench of whiskey came from the lawman's mouth. "Sheriff, you're drunk!" said Silvia as she slowly put her hands on Sheriff Wellman's chest to push him from her. All at once, the sheriff violently grabbed Silvia by both wrists and threw her to the ground. Everyone in the room screamed for the sheriff to stop. Deafened by drunken rage, he paid no mind to the pleas. Silvia tried to get to her feet. Wellman shoved her back to the ground and crouched over her. He pulled his fist far back and was about to deliver a harsh blow to Silvia's face when suddenly Octavia ran to Silvia's aide.

"Sheriff, please! No!' Octavia grabbed his arm.

Sheriff Wellman then pushed Octavia to the ground and rose from over Silvia. The brave widow rolled over and tried to quickly escape by scurrying on her hands and knees but the sheriff soon made his way to her. He gritted his teeth together and kicked her in the ribs. Octavia fell to her side and began screaming in agony.

Wellman reached down to grab a handful of Octavia's hair as he yelled, "You think you're stronger than me?" He jerked her head back by the hair and pulled her body around to face him. Wellman held Octavia's long brown hair and savagely punched her in the face.

Rusty rose up but fell back to the ground, still too weak to respond. The attack continued. Silvia got up and ran over to the sheriff. She kicked him in the back, then punched him in the face as he turned. Wellman threw Octavia to the ground and quickly turned and swung at Silvia. He knocked her to the ground and then bent down to continue his assault on her.

"Momma!" screamed Silvia's son, Michael as he ran to her. The boy grabbed Sheriff Wellman by the shoulder.

"Get off of me, boy!" screamed Wellman as he backhanded the child. Michael fell and rolled across the floor.

"Michael!" screamed Silvia as she lay on the ground with blood dripping from the side of her mouth. Michael lay there crying. Wellman turned back to Silvia, fists swinging.

Fred stood at his cell door screaming at the sheriff since the attack started. "Wellman! You're a dead man when I get outta here! You hear me? I'm gonna kill you!"

Sheriff Wellman suddenly stopped. Everyone screamed and cried–except Fred. Wellman lowered his fist and turned toward Fred.

"Yeah! You heard that didn't you, big boy?"

Wellman squinted his eyes and gritted his teeth.

Fred smashed his hands against the steel bars. "Come over here and fight me! I swear! I'll tear your head off, Wellman!"

The sheriff rose up and stumbled over to Fred's cell. "You think you're gonna kill me?" A smirk grew across Wellman's face.

Fred pressed his face as far as it could go through the cold iron bars. "That's what I said, you coward! Come in here and fight me! Just shows what kind of a man you are, beating on women and children!"

Sheriff Wellman laughed, "Fred, you're the one that's gonna be dead!" He slapped his chest. "By my hands! You sure can talk inside that cage, like some circus-animal! Well, we'll see how good you talk with a rope around your neck, hanging from a tree!"

Fred was overcome with anger and threw a punch at the sheriff through the bars, but missed.

"Whoo! Easy there Freddy-boy, you about got me." laughed Wellman. "You know what? You may not be hanged! I might not get the privilege." He turned and pointed to the window. "Those monsters out there might just bust through that door and eat us all! Or you never know, Deputy Hansen and his band of morons may just walk through the door and say, 'We killed them all boys!' But I really doubt that one though."

Fred stood there with fists clinched. Everyone else huddled together, fearful of Wellman's next move. The sheriff looked at Dr. Richards' body laying in the cell next to Fred's. He shook his head and stumbled through the open door and into the cell with the body. Fred watched Wellman enter the cell; once he lost sight of the sheriff he looked at everyone else to watch their eyes.

Sheriff Wellman walked over and stood beside of Dr.

Richards' body. "Poor guy. He must be the stupidest dead man there is! This man right here is the very reason all of y'all are in here crowding up my jailhouse!" Wellman looked at the green, blood-stained blanket that covered his body. Everyone in the building sat still. Wellman reached toward the part of the blanket that covered Dr. Richards' head. He grasped the fabric and jerked the cover from the doctor. Wellman stood there looking at Gene for a moment. Skin shone pale-blue; dark veins visible beneath the skin's surface. Wellman cringed at the sight of the bloodless bite mark gouging the man's arm.

The sheriff nodded his head and said, "It's a good thing you're already dead, Doc. Cause I'd have to kill you anyways now." Wellman paused for a moment as he looked up at the nearest wall. He lowered his brow and said, "That's just what I need to do." Wellman then turned toward everyone huddled together in the jailhouse. He took a couple of steps toward them as he reached for his gun in its holster. He removed the gun and aimed it toward the crowd. "I'm gonna kill you all!"

"Sheriff, please! Don't do it!" begged Silvia. Her eye was swollen shut and her lip still bled.

The sheriff stood just inside the cell, pointing his gun as he exclaimed, "Sorry folks, this jailhouse is overcrowded! And I gotta clean it out!"

Bella stood up and started toward the door in hopes of escaping.

"Hey you old hag!" yelled Wellman.

Bella stopped and slowly sat back down next to her husband.

"Ain't nobody getting out of here unless I say!" Frustrated, he bit his bottom lip. "Why do y'all keep trying to act like you're above the law? You're not! Ain't nobody above me! I'm gonna do what I wanna do around here, and I'll take whatever I want too!" Wellman then cocked the hammer back on his pistol. "I had every right to take that money from Reverend Hopkins! They didn't even ask me nothing about building anything here. Just went ahead and decided to do whatever they want in my town. That just ain't right!"

Fred heard the click of the gun's hammer as it was pulled back, ready to fire. He quickly tried to reason with Wellman. "Sheriff it's not them you want to kill! It's me you want!" yelled Fred from the other cell.

"Shut up over there! You'll get yours soon enough! I'm gonna let you watch the gun show first!" Wellman looked out of the corner of his eyes. "It's your fault everybody heard about all of this. It's your fault these people are gonna die, Fred." The sheriff aimed his gun at little Michael.

Silvia held her son tightly against her body. "Sheriff no! Please!" she screamed.

The others began screaming as well. The crowd was in a panic.

Octavia stood in front of her daughter, Susan and said, "Whatever happened, Sheriff, we can forgive you. Please don't do this!"

Bella stood by Rusty. He struggled to talk. "Sheriff, we don't know anything." Rusty took a deep breath. "You can't just kill innocent people."

Wellman slowly began to squeeze the trigger.

"Oh my goodness!" mumbled Rusty as his eyes looked past Wellman.

A burst of fire came from the gun barrel, and a single gunshot rang out inside the jailhouse. Everyone screamed a collective shriek of terror.

Even Wellman.

Fred glanced at everyone in the crowd trying to figure out who Wellman shot. No one seemed to be harmed, yet the screams continued.

"What's going on?" yelled Fred.

"He's got him!" replied Silvia as she glanced at Fred for a moment then back toward Wellman. She held Michael against her legs and made him turn his head to look the other way.

Suddenly another gunshot was fired–Wellman continued screaming. Fred then saw Wellman's gun land just outside of the cell door.

"Who's got him? What's going on over there?"

"It's Doctor Richards! He's up!" said Silvia.

Fred's eyes widened as he whispered, "Oh no!" He tried to think of something fast. "Close the door! Somebody shut that door!"

Silvia ran to the cell door. She watched as Dr. Richards held Wellman around his chest and head as he bit into his neck. Blood poured from the wound as the doctor ripped the meat from Wellman's neck and feverishly chewed it. Wellman reached out toward Silvia as she ran up, grabbed the iron bars and slammed the door shut with all of her might. Silvia stumbled back a few steps as she watched Gene pull another chunk of meat from Wellman. Gene pulled his head back while he violently shook it, trying to tear veins and cartilage apart from the rest of the body. Wellman's screams began to cease as he could no longer struggle with the doctor. His body became limp and fell to the floor. Gene continued eating away on Wellman's body.

"I'm gonna be sick!" said Octavia as she cupped a hand over her mouth.

"He's like an animal," said Silvia.

Everyone watched in a strange mixture of horror and fascination.

Bella said, "Come on, kids, let's go to the back room for a while," and took Michael and Susan by their hands. "You girls come with me too. Let me take care of those wounds."

Silvia and Octavia followed Bella to the back room.

"Fred, I just don't understand what's going on. Doctor Richards was dead." said Rusty.

"I don't know either." Fred looked back at the Bible lying on his bed. "The dead are coming back to life."

Chapter 9

"Don't they ever get tired," Ronald shouted as he and the others followed Sid through the inside of Betty's Restaurant.

"I'm guessing not!" replied the deputy.

The men stopped inside the dining area of the restaurant to rest for a moment. Felix shut and locked the door behind them. All of the men leaned on separate tables trying to catch their breath. Ronald walked over to a window that faced toward the jailhouse. He moved the stitched flower curtain and peeked out. "Everything looks pretty calm over there."

Sid scratched the back of his head. "I hope so."

Ronald continued looking at the jailhouse for a moment. Suddenly, a biter slapped a hand against the window, trying to get to Ronald.

Ronald screamed and jumped away from the glass.

The men stood silent as they heard more footsteps on the porch. Felix stepped to the back room and looked out of another window.

"This ain't good guys."

Sid went to the back with Felix. "What's going on out

there?" Felix stepped to the side to let Deputy Hansen look out. "No." He paused as he continued to look out back.

Some of the biters out back began walking to the front, but many of them still tried to force their way in through the back.

Ronald yelled, "Deputy! We've got biters out front now too!" He began moving tables in front of the door.

Sid glanced away from the back window and said, "They're surrounding us!"

"Deputy, neither one of these doors are gonna hold them out for long." said Felix.

Sid stood there pondering a plan. His gaze darted around the building.

Ronald muttered, "Deputy, there's too many of them!" He pushed his weight against the tables at the front door.

Sid began to breathe heavy. Panic reared its head.

Suddenly, a loud cracking sound came from the back door. The men stood there and waited for the town's deputy to think of something.

"What's the plan, Deputy? It's not gonna be long now!" said Felix.

Another loud crack sounded, quickly followed by three more. The front door bowed in. One of the biters outside smashed one hand completely though a panel in the wooden door. The men saw numerous bodies through the jagged hole.

Sid knew they needed to act fast. "Upstairs! Now!"

The deputy ran to the stairs in the kitchen area. Ronald looked at Felix, then shrugged his shoulders and followed Sid.

Felix watched in disbelief as the two of them ran upstairs.

"We're gonna be like sitting ducks up there,"

"Same thing down there, Felix." replied Sid as he

reached the top of the stairs. Another loud crack came from the back door.

Felix started up the stairs.

"I hate it when he's right."

The entire upstairs area was a single bedroom. One large wooden chest sat across the room from a neatly made iron bed with a small nightstand beside of it.

Sid ran over to the wooden chest and pulled it over. "Give me a hand boys!"

The other men ran over to the deputy and helped push the chest toward the staircase. Once they had it to the edge Sid said,

"Pull out all the drawers!"

Dave and Ronald pulled out the drawers and sat them all to the side. Once all of the drawers were ripped out, Sid gave the order to push. All of the men then pushed the large dresser down the stairs. It slid and hit the wall at the bottom of the staircase with a loud thud. It landed on its side, blocking a portion of the steps.

"Throw these drawers down there too," Sid said.

The men frantically tossed drawers down on top and around the dresser. Ronald ran to the bed. He pulled the mattress off and pushed the bed toward the stairs.

"That a boy! Let's get everything down there!" shouted Felix. The men grabbed the mattress and nightstand, then threw them to the bottom of the stairs.

Once everything was down, Sid ran to the window looking out the front of the building. He saw deceased friends still trying to force their way inside.

"That stuff is only gonna hold them down there for a little while," he said.

On the other side of the empty room, Ronald peered out the back window. "That's not good then, Deputy. They're coming in through the back now!"

Felix looked toward the staircase when hisses and

moans filled the downstairs foyer.

"What now, Deputy?" asked Felix.

Sid still watched out the front window. He stretched his neck to see the front door. "I can't see the door. The roof on the porch is in the way." A huge crash echoed over the sounds of the monsters downstairs. Shortly after, the moans amplified twice as loud.

Felix said, "I think they just broke the front door down."

Sid watched the mob standing off of the porch dwindle as they ran toward the door. "Yep, they're in."

"We're dead," Felix said.

"How high would you say we are?" Sid asked as he continued to watch the dead pour inside. "High enough to break our legs if we try to jump." commented Dave.

Felix looked at Dave and then said to Sid, "Deputy, that ain't gonna do us a bit of good. We can't run with broke legs!"

"We don't," vaguely replied Sid.

"What are you talking about, Deputy?" asked Felix.

"We don't break our legs! Look!" said Sid as he pointed down at the roof covering the porch. The men came over to look out of the window.

"That just might work!" said Dave.

"They're all gonna be inside distracted. So we just go out on the roof and quietly hang off the edge and drop to our feet. Then we'll have a clean break to the jailhouse!" explained Deputy Hansen.

"Then why are we standing here talking about it? Let's go!" said Felix with a laugh.

Sid raised the window and crawled out on the roof. He turned to help the others out. Once the last man, Dave, was through, Sid closed the window.

"Alright, now. Easy does it." whispered Sid.

Ronald was the first to go. Carefully, he lowered himself off of the roof. With his body fully extended he saw the chaos taking place inside the restaurant. The biters fought and tripped over one another to make it past the temporary wall the men made at the bottom of the staircase. He let go and dropped to the ground. No one spotted him, Ronald signaled for the next man to come.

Dave carefully made his way to the ground and signaled for the next. Felix cautiously eased to the edge and followed suit.

Just as Sid eased toward the edge, he was startled by a group of biters that managed to make their way past the wall of clutter and up to the window. He hurried as they broke the glass from the window and climbed out on the roof. Sid let go of his grip and dropped to the ground. He stumbled when he fell to the ground.

"C'mon!" he said as he jumped to his feet. The group ran toward the jailhouse.

The biters upstairs fell off the roof. The others downstairs noticed the men outside and ran out of the doors after them.

With the jailhouse now only yards ahead, the men gathered what strength they had left and ran as fast as they could to safety.

Felix yelled, "I hope they're expecting us back this soon!"

Chapter 10

"Rusty, are you sure you don't want to join us in the back? The children would really like to hear one of your stories," Silvia said in a kind and gentle voice. Her eye was blackened. The wounds on her face were bandaged by Bella, who treated everyone hurt by Sheriff Wellman.

"That's ok, Silvia dear. I'd just like to stay in here for now." Rusty sat behind Deputy Hansen's desk with fixated eyes on Dr. Richards.

The doctor had by then tore Wellman's arms from his torso, and completely ripped his upper body from his lower.

"What's happening to these people Silvia? Doctor Richards was a fine man. He died, but now look!"

Silvia glanced at Gene for a second and then back away. She felt her knees begin to buckle as she tried to push the gruesome image of the doctor eating away at Wellman's body out of her mind. " know, Rusty; it's something none of us can explain."

Rusty continued to stare blankly at the carnage taking place inside the cell. "You think it might be some kind of a sickness?"

Silvia slowly shook her head. "I don't know. It could be."

Rusty took his eyes away from the cell and looked at Silvia. "What if we all catch it from being in here with him?"

She put a hand up to her cheek. "My goodness, I hope not."

Rusty was silent for a moment. He looked over to Fred, who still sat on the bed in his cell, "Fred, what was Sheriff Wellman talking about? Right before Doctor Richards grabbed him, he was talking about taking money from the reverend."

"Wellman hired a posse to steal the money that Reverend Hopkins and his wife, Gwen was collecting to build on to the church. Gwen was in there on Friday getting the church cleaned up and ready for services early. Her and Reverend Hopkins was supposed to travel out of town yesterday. She wouldn't have had time to get it all done when they got back." Fred took a deep breath before he continued. "The posse wasn't expecting anybody to be in there on Friday evening, so when they came in to take the money, Gwen was there and they kidnapped her."

Silvia nodded her head. "Yes, I heard Gwen went missing yesterday."

Rusty looked back to Fred. "Did they find her?"

Fred rubbed the side of his unshaven face. "Wellman killed her."

Rusty and Silvia shook their heads.

Silvia looked at Fred as tears swelled up in her eyes. "And that's why he put you in here, isn't it? You knew."

"Yup. But that's the law for ya in this town."

Silvia shook her head as she walked to the keys hanging on the nail near Fred's cell. "The nerve of that man."

Just as Silvia reached above her head to grab the keys, Fred said, "Shh!"

Silvia stopped. She and Rusty looked at Fred.

"Do you hear that?" Fred asked about the faint sound outside.

Silvia and Rusty heard the same thing. Fred stood up and walked to his cell door. He leaned his ear between the bars.

"What is that?"

Everyone in the back room ran out to see what was going on.

Silvia looked out of the window. She saw Sid waving his arms as he saw her look out. "Thank the Lord! It's Deputy Hansen and the others! They're heading this way!"

Octavia ran to the door and raised the blockade to let them in.

"Goodness, look at them all!" said Silvia, bewildered by the number of walking dead pursuing them. "They're getting close, open the door!"

Octavia ripped the door open as the four men thundered inside.

"Shut it! Shut it!" screamed Deputy Hansen. Octavia slammed the door shut and Silvia quickly slid the blockade back in place.

The hungry horde smashed into the thick steel door. The groans outside was loud. The children covered their ears and started to cry. Dr. Richards slammed himself against the cell bars as he heard the ruckus.

Sid looked at everyone in the room. "What happened in here?" he asked, shocked by Octavia, Silvia, and Michael's wounds. The four men were completely taken back by what they saw.

"Silvia! Who did this to you and Michael?" demanded Ronald as he saw his family's injuries.

Silvia began to sob as she said, "The Sheriff done this to us all!"

The men then looked in the cell with Dr. Richards.

"Doctor Richards is one of them now?" asked Felix.

Sid quickly started shaking his head. "Whoa, whoa, whoa! Hold on? What happened while we were gone?"

Fred spoke up, "It went like this Deputy, Sheriff Wellman was in the back getting drunk, then came out here running his mouth on everybody and went off on a drunken fit. He walked over in that cell, looked Doctor Richards over for a minute." Fred stopped for a second, as he gathered his thoughts. "Now keep in mind, he was still dead at this point. Wellman turned and was about to shoot everybody when the doc saved everybody by grabbing him."

"It's a good thing you guys got this door closed." said Sid as he watched Dr. Richards eat Sheriff Wellman's remains.

"He's like an animal!" said Dave.

Fred let the men observe Dr. Richards for a moment. "What happened out there? And where's Steven?" he asked.

Still looking at Dr. Richards, Sid nodded and said, "It's bad out there. We were in Randal's Mercantile, with those people trying to bust down the door. We decided it was gonna be best if we tried to get to Whittlersfield and get some help. But when we made it to the gate, there was a big group of them right outside. We about ran into them, so we shut them out and just ran. You can't kill them either. We tried to shoot them dozens of times." Sid cleared his throat. "They got Steven."

"This ain't good." said Fred as he watched the men staring at the cell.

The four men stood there in disbelief as they reflected on what they had just endured, and seeing what happened to Sheriff Wellman.

Dave suddenly had a thought come to his mind. "Hey, since Wellman is dead, don't that make you the sheriff now, Deputy?" asked Dave.

Sid shook his head as he continued watching Dr. Richards. "No, actually the town is either gonna have to vote or appoint a new sheriff. It has to be done by the majority."

Felix looked around the room. "Um, I don't mean no disrespect or anything Deputy Hansen. I know about this whole democracy, majority rules thing. But based on what I seen out there–well, pretty much, the entire town's population is standing in this room. If not all, then definitely the majority."

Sid looked around at everyone as he realized the distressing truth of what Felix just said.

Ronald stood there with his arms around his wife and son. "He's right. You know what we saw out there. We're out numbered."

Dave spoke up once again, "So it's decided. I nominate Deputy Sid Hansen to be our new appointed sheriff."

Felix responded by saying, "I second that!"

"Alright, all in favor?" continued Dave.

The entire room spoke up with a unanimous "Aye".

"And all opposed?" The room was silent.

"Well, that's that. Congratulations Sheriff Hansen!" said Dave as he shook his hand.

Sid forced a smile. He wanted to be happy, but he knew the situation was grim.

"There's something I need to tell you all about."

Everyone could tell Sid had something on his mind. They all gave their undivided attention to their new sheriff.

"I'm sure you all know about the money Reverend Hopkins and Gwen were taking up to use to expand the building. And I'm sure you've all donated in one way or another to the fund that was supposed to be used to expand the building. Well, the truth about that is, the money was stolen."

Most of the people were confused by what Sid told them.

"Wellman hired some guys to rob that money. When they came in the church, Gwen was there. They kidnapped her. Wellman thought she was the only witness, so he killed her. I didn't know what had happened; but it was all behind my back!"

Ronald looked around, then back at Sid. "I can't believe Wellman would have done something like that."

The crowd was quiet. Rusty and Silvia already knew what Wellman had done.

Sid moistened his dry lips. "I know this probably came as a pretty big shock. I never would've known if not for Fred."

The crowd looked at Fred, who sat on his bed. Sid continued, "That's why Wellman had Fred locked up in the first place! Fred was trying to do what was right."

Fred looked at Sid.

"As my first official action as sheriff, Fred Douglas is cleared on all accounts he was accused of."

Sid walked over to the keys hanging near Fred's cell. As Sid unlocked Fred's cell door he said, "You're a free man Fred. And we could really use your help out there."

Fred continued to sit on the bed. "I can't help you."

Surprised, Sid tried to assure him everything was alright. "Fred, c'mon. We all know you didn't do anything wrong in the first place. As far as I'm concerned, you never done anything."

Ronald spoke up, "Fred, we all need you. You've always been there when we've needed you. And we need you now, more than ever."

Fred held the Bible up and exclaimed, "You don't understand! It's all right here!" Sid gave Fred a confused look.

"It's the signs! The end of time is here!"

Confused, Sid asked, "What are you talking about, Fred?"

"Don't you see?" asked Fred. He paused and looked around at everyone. "Everything that's going on with these people. The dead are coming back to life!"

Silvia's mouth dropped open as she said, "Oh my gosh! He's right! It's one of the signs of the end of time! Revelations."

Fred pointed at her and said, "Exactly! And there's nothing you, me, or anybody can do that's gonna stop that from coming!" Fred looked around; the crowd was silent as Fred's words settled on them. He breathed heavy as he looked around and lowered the Bible down to his lap. "So the best thing for us to do is just stay put for now." he muttered as he looked down at his feet.

Sid stood in the cell doorway, looking down at the ground. A gunshot rang out across town. Everyone traded gazes. They could hear the moans of the biters outside fade away as they all shuffled towards the sound of the gunshot.

After a moment Sid looked back to Fred and spoke. "Maybe you're right Fred. Maybe you're right." The newly elected sheriff placed his hand over his nose and rubbed down his face. He let out a deep sigh. "My family is still out there. My wife and my kid. They're still out there." He began to get choked up. Fred looked up at Sid, who was visibly upset.

Sheriff Hansen continued, "If this is the end or not I still want them with me. And I'm asking you Fred, as an old friend, please. I need you to help me get to them and bring them back here."

Fred thought to himself for a minute.

"Look Sid, there's some things we can't change." Fred examined his old friend's actions. He could tell this really meant something to Sheriff Hansen.

Fred fought with his own thoughts inside of his head. Memories of the times when he and Sid were together in a group of elite lawmen known as "The Good Boys". They spent many years working together, hired by the sheriffs and mayors of different towns, bringing in outlaws and other wrongdoers. Neither of the men stayed in contact much after the group split. All of the members left to pursue other interests in their lives.

Fred added, "And if that's true then–it's not gonna make much difference if I stay here or go. What's meant to happen is just that. Meant to happen." Fred walked out of the cell towards Sid. "We're all controlled by our destiny, but sometimes it's gonna take us to steer what way we get there." He held out his hand. "Let's go bring your family back here, Sid."

"Thanks again, old friend." said Sid as he shook Fred's hand.

Felix spoke up, "I'm coming with y'all."

Dave and Ronald both agreed to come with Sid and Fred as well.

"That's alright. I would rather you stay here and get rested. Ronald you need to be with your family. And Dave, I'd feel a lot better if you and Felix stayed with him to help protect the group; you never know what could happen." said Sheriff Hansen.

Dave replied, "Alright, Sheriff. You're the boss. You guys be careful out there, though. I want to see all of you back here safe." He patted Sid on the shoulder.

"Sure thing, bud." said Sid.

Fred wanted to see what everyone had been talking about this whole time. He walked over and leaned his head just enough to see the atrocious sight of Dr. Richards devouring Wellman's body.

"That's just sick," he said.

Sid put his hand on Fred's shoulder as he replied,

"Yep. And you're about to see a lot more of that same thing."

Fred watched as Dr. Richards savagely ripped meat and organs from the inside of Wellman's rib cage. The doctor's lips were covered with blood. His red teeth reflected in the sunlight coming through the small cell window. He pulled entrails from Wellman's gut and bit into the stretchy tissue.

"I just don't get it." muttered Fred.

"I know it's hard to see." said Sid.

"Well, yeah. But I was gonna say, how can he eat that much at one sitting? That right there is a lot to take in for one meal."

Sid couldn't suppress the grin as he shook his head.

"We're gonna need more guns, Sheriff." said Fred.

"Fred, it's not like you think out there. Our guns don't help at all."

"It'd still make me feel better though."

Sid walked over and got Fred's ivory handled pistol from his drawer. Fred took one of the .12 gauge coach guns from the gun rack beside of Wellman's desk. He broke down the barrel to check the bullet chamber; it was loaded. Fred slung the gun over his shoulder and around his back with its strap. Sid handed Fred his belt. Fred then wrapped the belt around his waist and placed his gun in the holster.

Sid gave Fred a pouch full of .12 gauge shells and said, "If you're gonna be packing that, then you might as well be packing these too."

As Fred hung the leather pouch around his empty arm he said, "Yeah, what good's it without, huh?"

Sid grabbed his pistols and extra bullets. He walked over to the door with Fred.

"You guys get back here quick." said Felix.

"We'll be back soon." replied Fred as he slid the blockade. He looked back at Sid and asked, "You ready?"

The sheriff nodded.

"Alright, let's get them back here." said Fred as he opened the door. He looked both ways before running out. Sid followed as he told Ronald, who was standing at the door,

"Keep this door closed till we get back."

Sid followed Fred. Ronald closed the door and slid the blockade back in place.

"I sure hope they find them." said Dave.

Chapter 11

Fred eased up the nearest alley.

"Sid, you never told me there was so many of these people."

"Well, I figured you could tell the size of the matter when everybody was talking about us being the only ones left in town." Sid checked behind them to see if any of the biters were following them. "Whatever you do Fred, try not to fire your guns unless you feel you absolutely need to. They can't be taken down by our bullets."

Fred just shook his head. "That's just crazy."

"Nothing is making sense around here."

The two came to the end of the alley. Fred's eyes were wide as he looked at the path ahead of them.

"This ain't gonna be good."

The street was filled with the undead. Each one walked about aimlessly; bumping into objects and stumbling around as garbled moans came from their mouths.

"It's like that all over town." whispered Sid. The two sat there for a moment. "Let's go this way Fred. We need to avoid them at all costs." Sid turned and headed back down the alley. He stopped at the edge of the building to make sure none of the biters noticed him.

"We're gonna have to crawl a little." Sid got on his hands and knees and crawled under a porch on the front of the next building. Most of the buildings in town had porches on the front, and Sid was going to use that to his advantage.

The two made their way under the first porch by crawling along on their bellies.

"You alright back there, Fred?"

"Yeah, I'm great." He wiped a spider's web off his face.

Sid looked at the next porch. "The next one's gonna be a little more tricky." The bottom was enclosed with wooden lattice.

"I'll keep an eye out for you." said Fred.

Sid checked the area around them just before he scurried to the next porch. There were some biters up the street and others behind them, but they all seemed oblivious to Sid and Fred.

Sid made his way to the next porch. He pulled on a section of lattice at the side next to the building. Fred watched the area around them. The wood popped as he tugged at it. Sid tried not to draw attention to himself. At last he wiggled the small section of lattice away from the porch. It made an opening just big enough for the men to squeeze through.

"Wait there, Fred. I'm gonna crawl to the other side and get it loose before you come in here, just in case." whispered Sid.

Fred watched Sid crawl to the other side and grab a section of lattice and start to pull it apart. He heard the sounds of shuffling feet and looked ahead at the ghouls roaming in the distance. Fred checked again behind them. Everything seemed to be going well. Fred watched the biters for a moment. He thought about how they behaved like animals. He still hadn't seen one of them actually attack someone, but from the stories he heard and the sounds coming from Dr. Richards, he knew what they were capable of.

Suddenly footsteps clumped above Fred's head. His stare was broken as his eyes darted to the cracks in the boards overhead. He saw a younger man shamble out of the door and onto the porch above him. The man stopped. Sid just finished opening up the last section of lattice. He turned and whispered, "Fred. I got it."

Fred put his finger to his mouth, signaling Sid to be quiet. The man whipped in Sid's direction. Fred pointed up; Sheriff Hansen then crawled over to look. Seeing the man standing above Fred, Sid eased back out of the man's sight and looked at Fred and moved his mouth to say, "He's right there." as he pointed.

Fred gave Sid an aggravated look as he mouthed back, "I know!"

Fred looked up as he watched the man limp toward the steps that led off the porch. Dust fell between the creaking boards with each step the man took. One of his legs seemed injured; he dragged one foot. As the man came to the first step, he struggled to step down. He slowly brought the injured foot down to the next step. Then the good foot stepped down on the next step. Fred and Sid looked at each other as the sounds of the man's steps came to a halt. All at once, he fell down the last two steps and landed hard on his back. Fred put a hand on his pistol as he prepared for the man to spot him. Sid was ready to come to Fred's aide if needed.

Fred watched the man as he lay there for a moment. His skin was pale, like all the others. Small areas of skin were missing from his face. His clothes were tattered and there was a large blood stain on the chest.

"Ughhh," moaned the dead man as he rolled to the side facing away from Fred.

Fred held a tight grip on his pistol as he watched the man rise to his feet. The biter turned and walked in the opposite direction Fred and Sid were heading. Sid let out a huge sigh of relief. He crawled back over to make sure there wasn't any more of the dead walking out of the building. Fred watched and waited for the signal from Sid.

It was clear; Sid waved his hand to Fred. Fred crawled out from under the porch and joined Sid under the lattice surrounded porch.

"That could've went bad in a second, Fred."

Fred smirked as he said, "I thought for sure he was gonna see me. Let's keep moving."

Sid and Fred continued crawling under porch after porch for a while. It was a far less noticeable way to get to Sid's house than taking the risk of walking through the streets.

The two finally arrived at the small white house. Sid lived across the dusty street from the saloon in town. His wife, Donna never cared much for the location, but the house wasn't far from the church, which was being used during the week as a school house; to her, that always outweighed the bad aspects of living there in the busiest part of town.

"Good. The front door is shut and the curtains are closed. Shew, please let them still be in there." whispered Sid as he and Fred looked from underneath a porch down the street.

Fred looked around them. "I'm sure they're fine, Sid. Let's not waste any more time. Let's get them back to the jailhouse where it's safe," he assured.

"I'd say the door is locked. So I'm gonna need you to cover me while I unlock it."

"I've got you buddy."

Sid and Fred quietly ran to the house. There were no

biters in sight, but both men knew there could be one anywhere. They approached the door and Sid immediately began unlocking it with his key. With a quick turn of the key, the lock clicked. Fred watched around them. Sid twisted the knob and pushed on the door–it wouldn't budge. He pushed a few more times.

"Augh!" He let out a sigh of disappointment. "It's jammed. There must be something against it."

Fred twisted his head and said, "That's a good sign."

Sid looked up at his roof and squinted his eyes. "Let's try the back." Fred and Sid hurried around to the back, keeping an eye out for any biters that lurked around.

Sid's heart sank when they made it to the back. The door stood wide open. They stopped in their tracks.

"Oh no," he muttered.

Sid and Fred both drew their pistols as they eased into the house. The first room they entered was the kitchen. It had been ram-shackled. The table lay overturned, with the chairs scattered and lying all throughout the floor.

Sid continued to ease through the house, into the hallway with Fred following. Their eyes moved about as they watched for any movement in the house. As the men entered the living room they discovered a very grizzly scene.

"James!" said Sid as he ran to his son. His son James lay on the floor in a pool of blood. His tiny neck, partially eaten.

"Is he breathing?" asked Fred as he knelt beside of Sid.

Sid held James in his arms. He raised James' chest to his ear.

"No." Sid cried, "He's gone Fred. My little boy is gone!"

Fred looked around the room. He noticed a woman's legs sticking out from the next room. "Sid."

Sid held James in his arms as he looked at what Fred

saw.

"No, no! This can't be happening!" He stood up with James and walked over to the other body.

Fred stood next to the woman. "Is that her Sid?"

Sheriff Hansen nodded as he knelt beside of her head. He ran his fingers through her hair and sobbed uncontrollably.

"I'm sorry Sid. I just wish there was something I could do." Fred looked down at Sid's wife. Large portions of flesh and muscle were missing from her arm and neck.

"She tried." cried Sid. "Donna tried to save herself and James. Why didn't I come here first Fred? What was I thinking? This was where I belonged! I should've put them first, above anybody else. They needed me to protect them!"

Fred wasn't sure what to say. He knew nothing he said would take the pain from his friend's heart at that moment. "Don't blame this on yourself. None of us knew what was gonna come from all of this. Nobody in this whole town knew that this was some kind of sickness that could go from one person to another. Not even Doctor Richards knew nothing about what was going on." Fred stood there a moment as Sid continued to mourn.

Two gunshots rang out from the saloon across the street. Sid paid no attention, but this put Fred on high alert.

"Sid, those were gunshots. As far as I know, those biters don't shoot guns."

Sid held his cheek down on James' head as he rocked him. "Just go, Fred. I need to be with my family right now."

Fred watched Sid and said, "Listen, I don't mean to sound this way, but you know what's gonna happen to them sooner or later. And I don't want you to be here when that happens." Sid was silent. "People ain't the same once they come back, Sid. When those two wake up, they're not gonna be anything like you remember."

Just then another gunshot rang out.

"Just go."

Fred stood there for a moment trying to decide what to do. "Alright, have it your way. There's people alive over there and they need help."

Sid wasn't about to budge. Fred started toward the kitchen. He stopped and came back over to Sid.

"Look, you stay here and take care of what you need to. I'll be back for you. You hear me? I'm coming back for you just as soon as I get them out of that building over there. If anything happens while I'm gone then you get yourself out of here and back to the jailhouse. You got it?"

Sid sat there and rocked his son and rubbed his wife's head.

"I'll be back, Sid. If they turn, then you run!" Fred ran out of the room while Sid sat there with his son's body in arm, and his wife's by his side.

Fred made it out of the kitchen and out of the house. He ran around to the front and saw a horde of the dead heading his way in the distance.

Fred said, "Here they come!" He continued to run toward the saloon. He ran through the doors and looked around. There was no one downstairs. Fred thought the silence was very strange, considering that just a minute before, someone shot a gun in the building. He thought for a moment that maybe he entered the wrong building. He checked in the back room; no one was there. He then dashed up the stairs.

He ran to a room at the end of the hall with its door open. As he turned to enter the room he was surprised to see a young woman standing at the other side of the room pointing a shotgun straight at him. Fred immediately dropped to the floor as the young woman fired a shot.

"Hey, hey! Take it easy, lady!" said Fred as he rolled onto his back.

"You're talking." She paused. "Say something else!" demanded the woman as she moved the gun's stock closer to her cheek.

"I'm not one of them!" yelled Fred.

The woman lowered her gun as she said, "Fred Douglas? Is that you?"

"Yes! I'm alive, I don't bite!" Fred looked at the young woman, she couldn't have been a day older than 16. Long brown hair flowed under the tan leather cowboy hat on her head. Dark brown eyes mesmerized Fred.

"My pa told me a lot about you. My name's Nataleigh." She broke down the barrel of her shotgun and reloaded.

Fred rose to his feet and walked toward her. "Well Nataleigh, I don't know if what your pa said about me was good or not but you're gonna have to come with me."

All of a sudden, Nataleigh snapped the gun back together and raised it up to her cheek and pointed it at Fred again.

Fred held his hands up and said, "Hey now, take it–"

"Get down!" yelled Nataleigh.

Fred ducked down. Nataleigh fired two quick shots right over Fred's head. He turned around to find two partially eaten bodies lying on the ground with huge portions of their heads missing. Fred then looked back at Nataleigh.

"Nope, Pa only had good things to say about you," Nataleigh said calmly as she reloaded her shotgun. "He said that he knew you were innocent, and Sheriff Wellman always had something against you. He believed you just had something on him, and that's the real reason he had you locked up."

Fred was in shock by both, the close encounter with the biters, and by Nataleigh's aim. He stumbled over to

Nataleigh as she finished reloading.

"So how'd you get out anyways?" she asked.

"Are they dead? And by dead, I mean are they gonna get back up?" asked Fred who was having a tough time gathering himself.

"Huh?" Nataleigh paused for a moment. "Oh. Yeah they're dead. They ain't getting back up. You've gotta shoot 'em in the head. I guess it destroys the brain or something. It's the only way to take 'em down. That I've found anyways." chirped Nataleigh.

As Fred walked backward toward Nataleigh, he kept his eyes on the two lying on the floor, "Shoot 'em in the head. Why didn't I think about that?"

The sound of footsteps thumping up the stairs came from just down the hall.

"You got bullets for those?" asked Nataleigh, referring to Fred's shotgun and pistol.

"Yep." said Fred as he patted the leather bag at his side.

"Good. Cause we're about to need them." Suddenly numerous biters burst into the room.

Nataleigh fired first. Fred ripped the shotgun off of his back and began firing. The dead swarmed the room, and as each entered the room, they were shot down.

The attack lasted for a few minutes, but seemed like forever to Fred. A total of ten biters were lying in a pile at the door. The attack seemed to be over.

"C'mon, I need to get you somewhere safe." said Fred as he grabbed Nataleigh's hand. She ran to the door with Fred.

"Where are we going?" she asked.

Fred had to step on some of the bodies in order to get out of the room. He turned to help Nataleigh over the pile of the dead.

"The jailhouse. There's already others there. It seems like the safest place to be right now." said Fred.

Just as Nataleigh stepped down on the floor of the hallway, a lone biter was coming up the stairs. His arms reached out toward them as he made a horrible hiss mixed with a loud scream. Fred pointed his shotgun with one arm while his other hand still held Nataleigh's. He pulled the trigger just as the man came within five-feet of the barrel. Blood and huge chunks of brain matter sprayed from the back of his head, covering the floor behind. The life instantly left the man's body; he fell forward and landed at Fred's foot. Dark blood oozed from his head and formed a large pool in the floor.

"It ain't the cleanest way." said Fred.

"No, it's pretty gross." replied Nataleigh.

Fred let go of Nataleigh's hand as he said, "Let's move, I gotta stop by and get Sheriff Hansen across the street." The two resumed running.

"Sheriff Hansen? What about Sheriff Wellman?"

Another biter shuffled into the building as the two were coming down the stairs. Fred raised his gun, and fired another headshot.

"They got him."

"Wow!" Nataleigh chuckled.

Fred and Nataleigh put their backs against the wall just before exiting the building.

"You know the streets are gonna be full of them now, don't you?" asked Nataleigh. Fred reloaded his gun.

"Yeah, I guess the noise is attracting them." Fred finished reloading and readied his gun to fire. "We're just gonna run in the house through the back, he's in there with his wife and son."

Nataleigh looked over at Fred with a huge smile. "They're alive?"

Fred shook his head, "No. Let's go."

The two ran out of the building. Three biters were outside. Fred fired a shot, and Nataleigh shot another.

Fred quickly moved to kill the next one as Nataleigh continued running toward the house.

As they rounded the corner of the house, they spotted a woman biter lurking around behind the house. Nataleigh shot the woman and reloaded her gun as she ran inside the house behind Fred.

They ran into the living room. Sid still sat in the floor beside of his wife while holding his son.

"Sid! We gotta go buddy, they're all stirred up out there." said Fred.

Sid looked up and was surprised to see Nataleigh with Fred. "Nataleigh?" Sid looked at the two of them for a moment. He knew Nataleigh and her dad very well. "Your dad?"

Nataleigh bit her bottom lip as she shook her head.

"Oh. This is just awful! What did any of us do to deserve this?" said Sid.

"Nobody did anything to deserve this, it's just something out of our hands right now. But sitting here isn't gonna help a thing!" said Fred.

Nataleigh spoke up, "Deputy Ha–I mean Sheriff Hansen, my daddy wanted me to go on and live. I could've sat with him after he was gone, but like he said, what good was that gonna do." Sid looked around at the mess in his home. "Don't you see, Sheriff? They would want you to go on too! Why would James want his daddy to sit here and eventually turn into one of those monsters?"

Sid continued to stare blankly as he rocked back and forth.

Nataleigh continued, "No, Sheriff." She pointed down at the bodies. "Cause that little boy and that beautiful woman were so proud of what you do. They knew your duty for this town was a great responsibility, and they understood that completely."

Sid shook his head as tears flowed down his flushed

cheeks. "I let them down so bad though! If I was here then I could've stopped this from happening to them!"

Fred leaned toward Sid as he raised one hand from his rifle and pointed at him. "No you couldn't, Sid!" Fred looked up at the ceiling and let out an aggravated sigh. "This was gonna happen whether you were here or not! Now the only people you'll be letting down is gonna be your town, us, and those two right there if you don't come back to the jailhouse with us!"

"He's right, Sheriff," said Nataleigh. She and Fred stood there with hopes that Sid might change his mind. Silence filled the room. The sounds of the undead started to grow louder outside. Nataleigh looked at Fred worried,

"They're coming." she whispered.

Fred looked back down at Sid. "C'mon, Sid! We gotta go! Now!"

The Sheriff looked up and tightly closed his eyes.

"Bah!" he cried. He took in a deep breath and rubbed his eyelids with the bottoms of his palms. "You're right. This isn't helping anything." Sid placed James beside of Donna, stood up and walked into the next room, a bedroom. He came back out with a large patchwork quilt. Sid unfolded it and placed it over both his son, and wife. "This is what they would've wanted." He took one more look at them just before he covered their faces.

"You're doing the right thing, Sid." said Fred.

After a moment, Sid rose back to his feet. He wiped his eyes once again and said, "Alright."

As he walked toward Fred and Nataleigh; Fred told him, "One thing before we go back out there."

Sid stopped and listened.

Fred handed him the rifle and bag of shells. "Aim for the head."

Sid was dumbfounded. "What?"

Nataleigh said, "I've just been aiming for their heads.

It seems like it kills them."

Sid shrugged his shoulders and said, "Hmm."

"Let's check around for more people that might still be alive before we get back." said Fred.

"Are you sure shooting them in the head works?" asked Sid. Fred and Nataleigh looked at each other.

"Yeah, it works." replied Fred.

The angry mob of biters staggered loudly down the street.

"We've gotta move!" said Fred as he motioned his head toward the door.

The trio made their way out of the house. Fred readied his pistol in his hands. Nataleigh peeked around the house. She could see the mob coming their way slowly.

"There's no way, guys." she said as she looked at the multitude of the dead.

Sid looked around the house too. "She's right, Fred. Even with guns, we're gonna have to reload in the middle of shooting. There's just too many of them."

Fred scratched his neck. "Let's go this way." Fred walked to the other side of the house. There was a side door leading into the house next door. Fred tried to open the door. "It's locked! Give me a hand, Sid."

Sid walked over and both men kicked the door until it busted open.

"Guys!" yelled Nataleigh. Two biters crept around to the back yard.

"Get in!" yelled Fred.

Nataleigh shot both biters then followed Fred and Sid inside. They ran all of the way through the house and into a living room. The large room was furnished with very expensive items. The front door was on the right side of the room and a window facing an alley on the wall across from them.

"We'll have to go out of this window and go down the

alley to the other end," Sid said. He raised the window and was about to lean out when he screamed, "Ahh!"

A biter that he didn't see near the house came staggering toward him. Sid fired a shot off just in time. The ghoul fell to the ground and Sid looked out the window again to check for more. He saw a wave of them coming down the alley toward the window.

"Here comes a bunch down here!" he yelled.

Loud thumps and bangs came at the front door. Fred ran over to look out of a large glass window next to the door. A large group of the dead was trying to enter through the front.

"Let's go back!" yelled Fred. The glass shattered as some of the ghouls forced their arms through the window.

Sid and Nataleigh followed Fred back through the house. The trio nearly made it back to the door they entered through when Fred ran into three biters and quickly put them down. More poured into the house through the open door.

"They're coming in that way." said Nataleigh as she shot two more of them.

"This was a bad idea." said Fred, commenting on his decision to enter the house. They turned around to run back through the house again. As they ran, Sid glanced around for a way out.

They passed by the kitchen and Sid stopped and yelled, "Whoa, hold on guys! In here!"

Nataleigh and Fred stopped and followed Sid into the kitchen. The sheriff had spotted a door in the floor leading down to the cellar.

Fred said, "Good catch, Sid!" He helped Sid lift the wooden door open.

"Hurry. They're coming." said Fred to Nataleigh.

She climbed down the ladder into the darkness. Another biter shambled through the hallway, past the kitchen. Sid climbed down. Just as Fred started to climb down, five biters suddenly came through the doorway toward him. He lifted the door higher as he turned to climb down. With one hand free, he drew his pistol from the holster and fired a shot. More biters moved into the room as he stepped down the ladder, closing the door little by little. Fred managed to fire the remaining bullets in his gun just before he narrowly shut the dead out.

The cellar was dark. The only light inside shined through the single window just above ground level. Sid walked over to the window and said,

"That door ain't gonna hold them out for long." He looked outside; the window was on the backside of the house. "I don't see any of them out this way."

Nataleigh replied, "I'd say they're all out front or coming through the side by now."

Fred walked to the window.

"Looks like this is gonna be our only way out." said Fred as he looked out with Sid.

Sid turned his shotgun around and held it by the barrel.

"We're gonna have to get out of here."

Fred stepped back as Sid drove the butt of the shotgun through the window; the glass shattered. The sheriff eased his head outside.

"It's clear." said Sid. Fred used his pistol to break away the remaining glass from the frame. He placed his hand on the window frame and pulled himself up and out.

Once Fred was up, he checked around again to make sure nothing was around.

"You go next, Nataleigh." said Sid while propping his shotgun against the wall.

Nataleigh handed her shotgun up to Fred. Fred then reached his hand down to pull Nataleigh up. Once up, she took her gun and watched out as Fred helped Sid up.

They still heard the biters inside the house.

Nataleigh looked in her bag. "I'm getting low on ammo guys."

"Same here." said Sid.

Fred nodded and knew what they needed to do. "Let's get back to the jailhouse. We'll have to stay low and try to be noticed as little as possible." said Fred.

"There's not many of them this way, let's just take the long way back." suggested Sid. Everyone agreed. The three of them started on their way back to the jailhouse as quietly as they could.

Chapter 12

"The sun's gettin' pretty low," Ronald said as he peeked outside for what seemed to be the hundredth time.

"Come sit down, honey." said Silvia. "They'll be back soon."

Dave sat against the wall next to where Ronald stood. "Yeah Ronald, you know how it is out there. Sheriff Hansen's smart, he'll figure out a way around the biters." he said.

Ronald continued to look outside. "Yeah, you're right. He's got Fred with him too." He walked over and sat next to his wife and son.

"Is he ever gonna stop eating?" asked Felix as he looked back at Dr. Richards, who had nearly eaten every bit of flesh and meat from Wellman's body. A small amount of skin and meat covered the fallen sheriff's face and neck, revealing a portion of the spine that attached to the base of his skull. Gene had ripped away Wellman's eyelids and most of the meat around his eye sockets, leaving a terrible, wide-eyed look of horror on Wellman's face. The rabid doctor tore apart the fabric covering Wellman's torso. He chewed through the skin and fat to the meat concealed deep inside his large body. Blood smeared the floor and walls inside the cell in crimson swirls and splashes.

"He's almost eaten every bit of him." said Felix.

Octavia covered her daughter's ears and said, "Felix, please."

Felix covered his mouth. "Oops!" He looked at little Susan. "I'm sorry."

Silence settled across the room. Dave got up and paced the floor as he hummed a church hymn. Bella sat with Rusty on Fred's old cell bed while she quietly sang the song with Dave. Ronald sat on the floor next to Silvia and Michael with his back and head resting against the wall.

"Mommy? I'm hungry." said Michael.

Silvia rubbed his head. "I know, baby. We'll get you something real soon." She knew that getting any kind of food was out of the question, but refused to admit that to her son.

Minutes passed by as everyone sat there, occasionally talking amongst one another. A light pecking came from the door.

Ronald looked at everyone. "Is that them?" he whispered. There had been a few ghouls pass by the jailhouse and bump into the door as they stumbled by.

Ronald stood up walked to the window. A heavy pounding came from the door. He looked out and saw Fred standing there. He couldn't see anyone else. "It's them! Open the door."

Felix ran over and opened the door. His face turned from a smile, to a look of sorrow as he saw Sid standing there without Donna and James. The three hurried inside. As Felix closed the door, Ronald and Silvia looked at Sid and back to Felix. Octavia buried her face in her hands as she began sobbing again as she realized Sid wasn't able to bring back his family. Bella and Rusty walked out of the cell. Bella glanced between Sid and Nataleigh. She smiled at the sight of Nataleigh, but her smile faded as she looked back to Sid.

Ronald looked sorrowfully at Sid. "Sheriff, couldn't you find them?" he asked.

"Yeah, we found them." He took in a deep breath. "The biters had already–"

Bella quickly walked to Sid and grabbed his hands. "I'm so sorry. I truly am." she said while patting Sid's hand.

Felix walked over to the sheriff's side. "Sorry. I know how you feel and I share your pain. I lost my wife and child too."

Octavia was overcome with grief as she continued to sob into her hands.

Sid fought back tears as he said, "Thank you all."

Ronald and Silvia stood up. "Sheriff," Ronald cleared his throat. "You know we're all here for you."

"I really do appreciate it, y'all. It means a lot." Sid paused for a moment. "Fred found Nataleigh here though." Sid wanted to take the attention off of him and dodge the conversations of his family.

Silvia hugged Nataleigh as she said, "Thank God you're okay." While still embracing her, Silvia leaned back as asked, "Your poor father didn't make it, did he?"

Nataleigh shook her head, "No, Pa didn't make it through."

Silvia embraced her once again. "I'm so sorry, Nataleigh."

All of a sudden Fred raised his gun and shot Dr. Richards in the head. Everyone was startled and screamed.

"Hey Fred, what's wrong with you, man?" yelled Felix as he sat there with his hands on top of his head.

"Sorry about that everybody, but if you'll notice

Doctor Richards ain't gettin' back up." said Fred.

Everyone watched for a moment.

Ronald looked back at Fred and exclaimed, "He's not! How?"

"Nataleigh here showed me a little trick. If you shoot them in the head, they stay down."

Dave clinched his fists as he spoke up, "This is great! Now we've got a way to kill them."

Fred agreed as he put his pistol in its holster. "We do, but that's not gonna be good enough. We ain't got the bullets. Not even one bullet for each biter. There's still way too many out there."

"We've got to think of a plan." said Sid to everyone.

Fred continued, "Yeah, and this ain't something that's gonna fix itself. We're gonna have to do something about this now. Cause if we don't, then we'll either starve, or mess up and let them in."

Dave glanced at Fred and Sid. "But what if this does go away, what if we starve them, or they just eventually die out?"

Fred shook his head. "That's just not something I wanna sit around and find out."

Sid then said, "Fred's right, guys. If we wait to find out, they may still be going strong, and we'll be too weak to do anything about them. More people might get in town and then the gate would be open for them all to get out and spread even more."

"So what do we do?" asked Ronald. Everyone sat and pondered on Ronald's question.

Felix spoke up. "What if we go get help from Whittlersfield?"

"I don't know," said Fred as he looked at Sid. "Whittlersfield is half a day away, and that's on horse back. By the time someone goes there and back, who's to say the biters won't be in here by then? And that's only if someone manages to get out alive. In that case, we just end up losing another one of us."

Everyone fell quiet.

"Alright." said Fred. He crossed his arms and looked down at the floor. "Let's just go over what we know. These things eat people, and when somebody's bit, they turn into one."

"There's a lot of 'em!" said Felix as he held his hand in the air.

Fred pointed to Felix. "Yes. And the only way we've found to kill one is to shoot their head. But we're close to running out of ammo."

Felix threw his arms up, "We're done for. What else can we do but try to fight or wait it out?"

"I don't know" muttered Fred as he rubbed his bearded chin.

Ronald looked to Sid. "Hey! What about the coal mine?" he suggested.

"What about it?" asked Sid.

Ronald looked around at everyone as he explained his thoughts. "There's hundreds of cases of dynamite in there." he said. Fred nodded as a smirk grew across his face.

Ronald thought on his plan for a moment and said, "If we could somehow lure them inside the mine in one location with every explosive in that mine in them same place. Then have all of that dynamite go off at once, they'd be gone! There's no way they could survive something like that!"

Fred and Sid looked at each other and smiled.

"Ronald, that has got to be the most brilliant thing I have ever heard!" shouted Fred.

"Dave, you help with the planning of the mine, right?" asked Sid.

Dave nodded and replied, "Yeah."

"Think you could draw us a map of the tunnels inside." asked Sid.

Dave became jittery as he grinned and clutched his hands together. "It might take me a few minutes, but I'm sure I could. It's not very big at all."

Sid ripped a map of Hazel and the surrounding area off of the wall. "Here, use this." Sid turned it over and spread the large sheet of paper out on a desk. Everyone gathered around as Dave sketched out a rough drawing of the tunnels inside the mine.

After a few minutes Dave finished making the last line and said, "This is it."

Fred looked over the map and asked, "Okay. Now where is the dynamite located?"

Ronald replied, "There's a few rooms it's kept in that's set up inside the mine. The rooms are scattered though a few tunnels and they're all locked up, but I know right where the keys are." He began pointing at places on the map where the rooms were. Dave marked each spot with an "X".

"This is gonna take some time." commented Sid with a worried look on his face.

"Dave, Ronald, Felix, you three are the only ones that know anything about the inside of that place. You think you guys could put all of that dynamite in one spot, and get the detonator ready tonight?" asked Fred. The three men looked at each other and agreed.

"I'm sure we could. Our best bet would be to do it in shifts. Two men inside and one out to watch." said Ronald confidently.

Not completely satisfied, Sid looked to Fred with a look of worry and asked, "Alright, and how do you think we can get all of the biters in there at once?"

Fred pointed at places on the map as he explained, "I think it would be best if someone could run inside with the biters chasing them, have the detonator over here on the outside of this other entrance."

"Shh." Rusty could hear the sounds of feet shuffling outside of the jailhouse. Everyone stayed silent and listened as a biter made its way past the building.

With the biter gone, Fred whispered, "Most of them should still be inside this big area here, so that's where you guys can put all of the dynamite. Have the person run through the mine and out the other end. That's where the detonator will be. Have a group waiting there, when the bait comes running out, set off the dynamite." Fred looked up from the map and at Sid. "Most of them will be killed by the explosion, but there's probably gonna be some close behind the bait. So the others outside will have enough ammo to take care of the few that make it out."

Dave scratched his head. "This sounds really good. But how is one person gonna make that run all the way from, say the gate, to the mine and all the way through it without getting caught by them?"

"Well Dave, you're just gonna have to run real fast is all I know." said Fred.

Dave turned around in the seat and shouted, "What! Me?"

Fred chuckled. "Easy now, son. I'm kidding. The only way we're gonna pull this off is if we have a team of horses and a wagon."

Felix looked at Fred and said, "They ate every horse in town, though."

Fred nodded as he adjusted his hat. "Here's what we need to happen, Doctor Richards' place is outside of town. The gate is closed so hopefully none of the biters got too far. Sheriff Hansen drove Doctor Richards to Whittlersfield this morning, so his horses should still be in his barn. Now none of this plan will probably work unless those horses and wagon are still there; so we need to get there first. If they're there then everything else should fall into place."

Rusty stood with the others around the map. A smile stretched across his wrinkled face. "I believe this will work."

Octavia nodded. "I think so, too."

Everyone in the room exchanged smiles as the glimmer of hope they all held on to grew brighter.

"Let's move out then guys. Time's wastin'," said Sid as he clapped his hands together.

With a troubled look, Fred said, "Sid, it would probably be best if you could stay and protect everyone here. You've been through enough today."

Sid looked at the other men gathering guns, then back to Fred. "But Fred, I want to help."

Fred patted Sid on his shoulder. "You will be helping. They need a good trigger here in case something was to go wrong here."

Sid was reluctant to stay. He let out a sigh as he looked around, "Alright."

"It's okay Sid, you're not doing anything wrong." said Fred. "Nataleigh, we could really use you out there in case we run into trouble."

"I was hoping you'd ask!" said Nataleigh as she came to Fred's side.

Sid gave Ronald, Dave, and Felix the last of the bullets from the back room. "You're gonna need these."

Fred turned to Sid as he stopped by the door. "We won't be back until tomorrow. If everything goes right, watch for us around noon."

"Alright, be safe, Fred. This might be our only chance we get at this."

Ronald gave his son a hug and said, "Be good for momma, you hear me? I love you." He rose up to Silvia.

She was beginning to cry. "Don't worry sweetheart, I'll be back for you. I promise."

"I love you. Don't do anything crazy." she said and wiped away tears.

"I won't. I love you." He stepped back as she let go of his hand. Ronald walked to the door with Fred while still looking at her.

"Everybody, we'll see you all in the morning," said Fred.

Sid closed the door behind Fred.

Chapter 13

The streets were quiet. Fred assumed most of the biters still gathered around the house on the other side of town. The group followed close behind him as they sneaked closer to the gate.

They passed by the mill. The stream poured over the large wooden water wheel. The peaceful sound of the flowing water drastically contrasted the sounds of the dead that chased Ronald, Dave, and Felix past there earlier. Ronald looked at the mill and thought back to Steven. It was where Steven worked day in and day out. The pain in his screams after the biters grabbed him still gave Ronald chills.

They continued past the mill, toward a street that would take them straight to the gate. Fred stopped at the edge of a building just before turning down the dusty street. He motioned for the others to stop. Fred peeked around the corner of the weathered building. The glare of the setting sun made it difficult to see much down the road.

Fred placed his hand above his eyes and surveyed the horizon.

Dave whispered, "You see any of 'em?"

"It's clear. I'd say they're all still on the other side of town right now." Fred looked back at the others. "C'mon."

As they made their way past the empty buildings, Nataleigh let out a heavy sigh.

"I can't believe everybody is just gone. There ain't nobody left but us." She wiped a single tear from her face.

Felix jogged next to her. "I know. Usually there's people everywhere you look around here."

Nataleigh fought back more tears as she said, "That's gone now. I don't think Hazel will ever be the same."

They arrived to the massive wooden gate. Fred looked up at the watch tower located at the side of the gate. It was a wooden structure and stood just above the top of the wall, overlooking half of the town, and a couple of miles outside of town. Two wooden ladders stretched straight up to the watchtower; one on the inside of the gate, and the other outside.

"Nataleigh, would you mind staying up there in the watchtower while we go to Doctor Richards'. We're gonna need somebody posted here tonight anyways. We need an eye on the mine, just in case any of the biters are wandering around there." he said.

The coal mine was within sight beyond the town. The entrance sat at the top of a small hill. A large grassy meadow surrounded the bottom of that hill with a worn path of dirt made by the wagons coming to and from the mine.

"Yeah that's not a problem." replied Nataleigh.

"Us four will get to Doctor Richards, and if his horses are there, then we'll get back here before dark." said Fred.

Nataleigh was worried, "If any biters come around the gate, should I shoot them?"

Fred shook his head. "Only if you're in any danger, and that's something like if they're climbing up the ladder.

We don't want a bunch of them to come around here on our account." he said.

She winked and replied, "Got it."

"Let's go, it'll be dark soon," said Fred and climbed the ladder. The others followed him to the top of the watchtower.

Once to the top, Felix looked around the inside of the watchtower and said, "Hey, this is alright." It was a very bare area with a solid roof built overhead. Walls were constructed all around the tower, standing waist-high with thick round logs placed strategically to support the roof. A tall wooden chair sat on the side that faced outside of town. A bed roll was rolled up, tucked away in the corner alongside a lantern.

Ronald unlatched the small door on the other side and climbed down. Dave and Felix went down next.

Fred said to Nataleigh, "If you do need anything, run like crazy after us."

She nodded. "I'll be alright, Fred. But don't worry, if I do need something I'll come find you."

Fred nervously fidgeted with his belt buckle. "If the horses are there or not, we'll be back. And if this works out, then I'm gonna let those guys set everything up. They know the coal mine better than anybody, so I'd just be in the way. Me and you will have to stay here and watch for them tonight."

"Sounds good. You'd better get to moving, Fred." said Nataleigh as she looked down and saw the other three men waiting impatiently.

"Yeah, I guess so." laughed Fred. He walked over to the ladder and just as he started to climb down Nataleigh said,

"Hey, Fred." Fred stopped and looked over at her. "Pa was right. You're a good man."

Fred was embarrassed a little, he grinned and said,

"I'll see you in a little while." He climbed down to the other men. Nataleigh closed and latched the small door as she watched the men leave. She turned to look at the town and let out a heavy sigh. A few biters roamed the streets. She hoped the men would return soon with good news.

Fred and the others traveled along the dusty road that led to Gene's house. Normally the sounds of the town could be heard from a good distance away, but the air held an eerie silence that evening.

As the men came around the last curve they saw the doctor's house surrounded by its white picket fence. The white paint on the house glowed a bright purple and orange from the painted sky of the sunset.

Fred approached the open gate with caution. The front door creaked as a light breeze moved it back and forth.

Walking lightly, Ronald whispered, "Think any of them are in there?"

"I don't know." replied Fred. They approached the gate.

Felix watched around them. "What if those kids got out of town earlier and came back here?" he asked.

Dave told him, "I don't believe the biters think like us. They act more like animals than anything."

"Animals still know where their home is though, Dave."

Ronald added, "That's true; I had an old hunting dog when I was little. He got lost from me in the woods for days. Finally he just showed up at the house again one day." The men stood just inside of the gate looking around for any sign of the dead.

"We don't know much about them right now. We're just gonna have to assume that anything they might do is possible." said Fred. "I see his wagon back there." He pointed toward the back of the house; it sat near the barn. The wagon was long and painted red. "Everybody just take it nice and easy, we can't take no chances right now." Fred crept through the front yard. The others mimicked his actions.

They all watched the area around them, and kept a close eye on the front door of the house. The grass grew over their knees; the evening dew made it stick to the ground with each step they took.

As they walked past the front porch, all eyes were fixated on the inside. A few chairs lay overturned, but there wasn't a lot of destruction inside; unlike other places they had seen.

Fred looked at the spots of blood in the grass. As he looked closer at the blood, he could see a clear trail that led toward the house. Fred looked on the porch and found more bloody spots that went inside. He suspected this was all the result of Gene running from his children; he envisioned the chase as he traced the path back to the road.

"The doors are closed." said Dave as he saw the front of the barn. "That's good at least."

The men walked through the yard beside of the house. They saw more of the backyard. A washing tub sat near the clothesline still full of water. They came around a corner and saw the home's backdoor standing open.

"Everything must've happened so fast." said Fred.

Ronald agreed, "It did in town, there was just nothing anybody could do. Everything went out of control in minutes."

At last they came to the barn door. Fred and Felix grabbed the handles and pulled them open. Dave stepped back as the doors swung open. He didn't notice the wood pile right behind him. All of a sudden Dave felt something quickly hit his boot. He was startled and screamed, then jumped forward. The men all stopped what they were doing and looked at Dave. He stood there with his gun pointed down at the woodpile.

"Dave, what happened?" asked Ronald. Just then they heard a rattling sound.

"It's a rattler, Dave. Don't shoot." said Fred. Dave could see the snake coiled up next to the logs. He was about to pull the trigger.

Ronald yelled, "Dave! Don't!"

Fred tried to explain, "If any biters got out of town while the gate was open, they're gonna hear that thing go off! They'll be on us in no time out here!" Dave lowered his gun as Felix stepped into the barn. He came back out holding a garden hoe. With a quick swipe, Felix chopped the snake's head off.

"See there, no noise, no biters," said Felix as he handed the garden hoe to Dave.

"Did it get you?" asked Fred. Dave put his gun and the garden hoe on the ground. He pulled his boot off to check for any bites.

"I don't see nothing." he said.

Fred watched Dave as he looked over his leg. "Does it burn anywhere on your leg?"

"No. It didn't get all the way through my boot."

Felix threw his hands up and commented, "What is it with this place and things biting everybody?"

The others walked inside the barn while Dave put the boot back on. He lifted his foot up to put it inside of the boot, then stopped as his eyes were drawn to the snake's body; he gazed at it. Its head lay about a foot from the rest of its body. It was uncoiled and making slow movements, he knew that a snake's body still moved a little like that after its head was cut off, but there was something about it this time–he had an idea. Dave dropped his boot while the snake's body moved. He knelt down to pick up the garden hoe. He just couldn't pull his eyes away from the snake.

Upon entering the barn the men saw both of Gene's horses standing there in their stalls.

"Yes!" said Fred as a feeling of great relief came over him.

Felix stood there and said, "I have never seen two horses look as good as them two right there."

As they led the horses from their stalls, Dave walked into the barn with the garden hoe; his boot was still off of his foot. He looked around at the walls.

"You alright Dave? That snake didn't get through your boot did it?" asked Ronald. Dave looked at the various garden tools that hung on the barn walls.

"No I'm fine." He looked at Felix. "You're right, ya know." Felix looked around at Fred and Ronald with a confused look on his face. "You know, no sound, no biters. Remember?"

"Yeah?" replied Felix.

"Well, look." said Dave as he pointed at the tools hanging on the wall. The men looked at the various tools on the wall. Among the tools was a scythe; it had a long, thick wooden handle with curves strategically placed at one point, with a large curved blade on the end of it. It was designed to cut wheat by the farmer swinging it while still standing. Also amongst the tools were two sickles. They were used for the same purpose as the scythe, but these were much smaller; wooden handles were small enough to fit only in one hand. The blades on the sickles were not as wide. They came up from the small handle and curved dramatically to a very sharp tip; it was in the shape of a question mark.

Dave took the scythe and sickles off of the wall and felt of their blades. Both were very sharp and had never been used. "Doctor Richards always talked about starting a farm, but he never could find the time." he said. He turned toward the men and asked, "Think these would be tough enough to go through a person's neck?" The others could see where Dave was going with his idea–and they liked it.

"Dave, that's probably the smartest thing that's ever come out of your mouth!" said Ronald with a laugh.

Dave laughed as he swung the sickles, "Ya think so, huh?" Dave was proud of his idea.

Pleased with Dave's discovery, Fred said, "Let's get these horses hitched up and get back to town guys. It's almost dark out now." The men had the horses hitched to the wagon in no time. Dave loaded his new weapons in the back and climbed in. Felix sat in the back with Dave. Fred then took the reins while Ronald sat next to him up front.

Fred said, "He-yah!" and gave a gentle tug on the reigns. "Everybody just keep a lookout around us. There could be biters anywhere."

The men went over the plan for the night quietly as they traveled down the road to town. The sky faded to black, and the glow of the moon hung just over the horizon. The trip back to town seemed to be very lonesome; the silence still seemed so strange.

Fred pulled the wagon near the gate as they arrived back to town. Once the horses stopped, he handed the reigns over to Ronald.

"Here ya go, Ronald. Me and Nataleigh will watch for you. You guys remember what to do if you need anything, right?" he asked.

Ronald nodded and said, "Yep, set off a stick of dynamite."

"Alright, meet us back here at noon." said Fred.

Ronald told him, "We'll be here. First thing we're gonna do is get the lanterns and things ready before we go inside."

Fred climbed off of the wagon. "Y'all be careful over there." He turned and climbed up the ladder of the watchtower. Ronald started the horses on their way through the field and up to the coal mine.

Fred got to the top of the ladder. Nataleigh leaned against one rail, looking over the town. He softly said, "Hey, you awake over here?" He reached his arm over the door and unlatched it.

Nataleigh turned around and said, "Hey." She smiled. "How'd it go?"

Fred stepped inside and latched the small door back. "Good. Both horses were there and so was his wagon. The others are on their way to the mine now." He joined Nataleigh on the other side and leaned on the rail beside of her. "What cha looking at?"

"Just the town." she said with a sigh.

Fred looked down and saw a few biters wandering around below the watchtower. "I see we've got some buddies down there."

Nataleigh smiled as she watched the biters and said, "Some company, huh?"

Fred laughed.

Nataleigh pointed at the old man wearing a hat. "You see that one right there?"

"The one with the hat?"

"Yeah. He was one of my pa's good friends. His name was Kurt, but everybody always called him Stoney. I never did know why."

Fred nodded, "Your pa was a pretty popular guy."

With a half-smile Nataleigh said, "Yeah. He had a lot of friends."

Fred was quiet as he watched the man limp around for a moment. "Where were you when your pa died?"

"I was there. He wasn't but a few steps from me. One

of the biters just ran at us. It chose him for some reason. We didn't have any guns or anything at the time. He just told me to run. So I did."

Fred wasn't sure of what to say. "He wanted you to be okay. That's just what dads do."

Nataleigh looked at Fred. "Do you have any kids, Fred?"

"Me?" He looked out on the horizon. "Naw, I ain't got no kids."

"Wife?"

Fred laughed, "Nope. Ain't got one of those neither."

Nataleigh turned her head to Fred. "Why not? Just seems like that would be a lonely life."

Fred shook his head. "I just never stayed in one place for a long time. A man makes a lot of friends that way. A lot of enemies too, I guess you could say." Fred smiled. "Hazel is where I was born, so it's the place I keep coming back to. But I wouldn't really call it home."

Nataleigh stared at Fred for a moment as if examining him, "Why are you running, Fred?"

Fred continued watching the biters below them. He had a confused gaze as he said, "Running? I wouldn't say that I'm running anywhere."

Nataleigh placed her hand on her cheek and leaned her elbow on the rail. "It just seems like you're running away from something. No wife, no kids, and you never stay anywhere for long. Not everybody does that you know."

Fred rubbed his hands together. "Well everybody don't shoot like you do, either. Where'd you learn to shoot like that?" asked Fred.

She smiled. "Pa taught me. He'd take me out and let me shoot his guns all the time; ever since I was big enough to hold one up by myself."

Fred raised his eyebrows. "Wow, that's pretty

impressive." He walked to the other side to look toward the mine. Nataleigh watched Fred as he leaned on the rail on that side. She followed Fred over and stood beside of him once again.

As she looked toward the mine she asked, "Do you think this whole thing will work?"

As Fred exhaled he scratched under his chin. "I hope so, cause if it don't then we've not got much else to choose from."

Nataleigh nodded. "I know."

Fred and Nataleigh continued talking through the late hours of the night. Fred continued to dodge her questions about his past. Nataleigh sat in the chair while Fred leaned against the rolled up bed roll.

"Why won't you tell me anything about yourself? Pa always talked so highly of you. How did he know so much?" She paused. "I mean, I know everybody has heard about all of the good deeds you've done, but Pa knew so much more than just that stuff."

Fred let out a deep sigh as he started saying, "Did he ever tell you my pa used to be a preacher?"

Relieved to finally get a little out of him, she said, "Yeah, he told me about that. I guess that's why you carry your Bible with you everywhere, isn't it?"

He looked at her with a smile. "Yep, my pa really meant a lot to me and everything he taught me." He paused as he continued to smile at her. "Your pa was in his congregation."

She twisted her head in amazement. "Really? He didn't tell me that. Did he stop preaching or something?"

"Something like that." Fred said somberly.

She looked compassionately at Fred and pleaded, "Fred, just tell me."

He hesitated for a moment. Fred always had trouble opening up to people. "Well, when I was about ten I rode home with my ma and pa one evening. A couple of guys stood beside of the road. They flagged my pa over, and being the kind of guy he was, Pa pulled over to see if they needed any help. Both men had guns, and they told Pa to give them his money."

Nataleigh was surprised. "Oh. Bandits?"

Fred nodded as he timidly looked at the wall. "Well Pa only had twenty-five cents to give the men. They wanted more but he didn't have it. One of them walked over and yanked ma off of the wagon. He held the gun to her head and told Pa he would shoot her if he didn't hand over any more. Me and Pa tried to stop them."

Nataleigh listened to every word. "Did they kill her?"

Fred reluctantly said, "No, they turned the gun on Pa. They killed him first. I was so full of anger; I came after that man holding Ma. The other guy shot me in the back."

Nataleigh put her hand over her mouth.

"That's when I blacked out. When I woke up I was in a stranger's house. The man told me him and his wife found me and dad lying in the middle of the road. They kept me there for a while until I was a little better."

Shocked by what Fred had just told her, Nataleigh asked, "Where was your ma?"

Fred uneasily rubbed the back of his neck. "Some people found her body on the river bank one day not too long after. I've been by myself ever since. All I wanted after that was to find those two men that killed my ma and pa."

"Did you ever find them?" asked Nataleigh, expecting a proud yes to come from Fred.

"Never did." Fred sat there for a moment. "I got with a posse later on, hoping to find them like that. After a few years, we gave up looking. We helped some other folks while we were together. But I've just been by myself ever since."

Nataleigh was speechless. "I–I just don't know what to say. I had no idea."

Fred pulled a splinter from a board at his side and gently tossed it in front of him. "Ah, there's not much to say, really. I just try to help people out. Not for the glory, I just feel it's the right thing to do. You know, kinda like what Ma and Pa would want me to do."

"You ever try to run for sheriff anywhere?"

"Nah. I've never been much on all that politic slop. There's just too much corruption in it, and I think people will just never trust someone like that. I figure working for myself is easier, I can play by my own rules."

Fred and Nataleigh continued to talk through the night. Fred had never opened up to anyone like that before. He had always kept to himself when it came to emotions and his past.

Chapter 14

With noon only an hour away, Fred watched for Ronald and the others on one side of the watchtower, while Nataleigh watched the town from the other.

"I hope these two leave before everyone gets back." said Nataleigh. Two male biters still wandered around below the watchtower. Many came and went during the night.

"At least it's not a bunch of them."

A small dust cloud started to rise in the distance, coming down the hill from the mine. Fred strained his eyes to see in front of the cloud.

"They're early." said Fred. Nataleigh walked over by his side and saw the dust cloud stretching toward them.

"Good." She stood there a moment as they both watched. "To tell you the truth, I'm pretty nervous about this."

"I understand. We all just have to stick together in this. It's the only way we're gonna get our town back."

Nataleigh looked at Fred. She was surprised by what he just said. "Our town? I thought Mister Fred Douglas doesn't stay in one place for too long," laughed Nataleigh.

Fred smiled and shook his head, "You know what I mean."

As the wagon came closer they could see that all three men made it through the night. Their faces and clothes were very dirty. Fred and Nataleigh climbed down the ladder to greet them.

At the bottom, Nataleigh waved at the men as they came close. Ronald led the horses near the gate before bringing them to a stop. Dust swirled around them as Fred said,

"Welcome back boys."

The men all had very concerned looks on their faces. Ronald looked at Fred and told him,

"We've got a problem Fred. A big problem."

Fred's heart dropped, his worst fear was that one of them would come back and say something like that.

"What is it?" asked Fred.

"It's the exit; there isn't one." said Ronald.

A cold chill rushed through Fred's body. "What do you mean? I thought there was one already made?"

Dave sat in the back of the wagon. "There was. But now it's blocked off, the ceiling collapsed near the exit. There's no way of making it out the other side."

Fred didn't know what to say, he was trying to think of their next move.

Ronald added, "Fred, we went ahead and set everything up, though. All of the dynamite is in place. The main tunnel runs straight into the large cavern where we put it all. It's the same spot we planned, there's just no way of getting out now."

Nataleigh looked at Fred, and then looked up at the other men. "What about the detonator? It was supposed to be outside the other exit wasn't it?"

"It was supposed to. There was just no way for

somebody to lead all of the biters inside and make it back out. It's hooked up and ready to go in the cavern with all of the dynamite. We knew this would be our only chance to do this, so we decided to set everything up just in case," replied Ronald.

Nataleigh took a deep breath as she glanced at the men. "We can't do this then. We're gonna have to think of another way. We can't have somebody go inside and blow themselves up with those monsters!"

Everyone was quiet, they all looked at Fred. He stared at the ground, scratching his cheek.

"It's alright, guys. This is our only shot; we don't have any other options right now. We're gonna stick with the plan," he calmly said.

Nataleigh was shocked by Fred's statement. "Hey Fred! We can't lose nobody else! And we surely can't send somebody in there to die!" The other men couldn't believe what Fred was saying; Nataleigh didn't understand what the original plan was.

Fred looked at Nataleigh with an uncompromising gaze. "Nataleigh, we have to go through with the plan. You all don't have a choice, this is your town and I ain't gonna see you guys lose anymore of it!" said Fred.

Angrily, Nataleigh yelled, "I thought you said this was our town Fred? You stood up there a minute ago and said our town! That means you're included in this too!"

Fred stood tall as he quickly replied, "Yeah, I am. I'm the one who's gonna go inside the mine!" He stopped as an unfamiliar calm settled over him. "I ain't backing down from this. You all don't have any other way!" Fred turned to walk away.

Nataleigh saw then what Fred meant. She didn't realize that he was the one to set off the detonator. Nataleigh's mouth hung open as she watched him walk away. She jogged to Fred and grabbed his arm as she said,

"You can't do that! Why don't we just go get everybody out of the jailhouse and bring them here? We'll lock the gate and never look back at this place!"

Fred shook his head. "That would never work, Nataleigh. There's no guarantee that we would get everybody back here alive, we can't take that chance. Even if we did, the biters would get out eventually, then they would be everywhere." He placed his hand on hers that still grasped his other arm. "I'm not gonna let that happen. This is gonna end here and now." Fred gently removed her hand, then turned and climbed up the ladder. Nataleigh breathed heavily as she looked back and forth between the men in the wagon and Fred climbing up the ladder.

"Ronald, tell him! He can't do this!" she begged.

Ronald was flabbergasted along with everyone else as they watched Fred climb the ladder. "I think he's made up his mind."

The men all jumped from the wagon. Ronald tied the horses to the gate while Felix and Dave went up the ladder. Ronald walked over to Nataleigh.

"Somebody has to do this Nataleigh. I know what you're saying, but Fred isn't gonna let one of us be the one to go inside." he said.

Tears swelled up in Nataleigh's eyes as she said, "Ronald, why can't we just try to fight them or run away? We can lock this gate and just get out of town."

"I don't wanna see him do this either, or anybody for that matter. These things are tough and if we don't do something to get rid of them now, then who knows what might happen if this spreads to other towns. We might not have another chance like this."

Nataleigh didn't like the plan, but she started to understand the severity of the situation. She wiped her eyes and looked up as Fred unlatched the small door to the watchtower. "Shew, I just don't get why this happened."

"None of us do. That's probably the scariest part about it all–not knowing anything." Ronald patted Nataleigh on her back. "C'mon, let's get up there with the others."

Nataleigh wiped her nose and agreed; she walked over to the ladder. Ronald followed her and the two of them climbed to the top with the others.

At the top, Fred, Dave and Felix were looking over at the town. Nataleigh and Ronald overheard the last part of Fred's conversation with them as they climbed inside the watchtower.

"We'll need all the help we can get from as many people as we can to hurry and push the rock in place." Fred turned to see the two of them just joining them. He gazed at Nataleigh as she wiped tears from her eyes. Fred felt a knot form in his stomach as he realized how much this really hurt her.

"What rock are you guys talking about?" asked Ronald.

Fred tried to set his feelings aside and explain his idea. "I think that once I get them all inside of the mine, we'll roll it in front of the entrance. That way none of them will be able to turn around if for some reason they wanted to." Fred took a deep breath. "So we need to get Sheriff Hansen, your wife, and Octavia to come back to the mine with us. Rusty and Bella should stay at the jailhouse with the kids, we need all the help we can get, but I don't want the kids to be out here. I don't believe Rusty and Bella would be able to help us much out here anyways."

Felix looked over at Ronald. "I told Fred that there was a huge rock right outside. So we don't have to go far to get one big enough."

Ronald concurred, "Sounds good." He walked over to the rail and looked below. The same two biters were still limping around. "And what about them?"

Fred looked over at Dave and asked, "Dave, you still got those sickles?"

Dave quickly turned to Fred and replied, "Yep, they're in the wagon."

With a grin Fred said, "We're about to find out the answer to your question about if they'll work." Fred looked over to Felix. "Felix, me and you will climb down there. I'll go first and see if I can take them out with the sickles so we don't attract more of them. If that works, we'll open the gate. The rest of you wait in the wagon. Dave, have your scythe ready cause when we ride through town we'll need to keep them away from the wagon." Dave nodded. "Ronald, you drive the wagon." Then putting aside his feelings of remorse he looked to Nataleigh. "Nataleigh, I'm gonna need you to help get them stirred up and have them chasing the wagon by shooting your gun." Nataleigh was a little more on board with the plan but still wasn't comfortable with it.

"Okay," she whispered.

Fred looked back over the town. "We'll drive around town a couple of times to get them all after us. Ronald, we need to stay far enough from them but at the same time keep them close enough to see us. We'll put a little distance between us and them and we'll stop by the jail. I'll go in while you drive around once more. I'll get everybody else ready to catch the wagon on your next pass."

"I sure hope this works." said Dave, trying to be as optimistic as he could.

Fred leaned over and rested his arms on the rail. "It will. I'm not gonna let you guys down." said Fred as he stared out to the town.

They all climbed back down to the wagon. Dave handed Fred the sickles.

"Hit 'em hard, Fred." said Dave.

Fred smiled. He turned and went back up the ladder. Felix followed him. All the others got on the wagon.

"You two ready for this?" asked Dave as he looked at Nataleigh and Ronald.

Nataleigh was checking her gun to get it ready. "As ready as I'm ever gonna be."

Chapter 15

"Man those things are ugly!" said Felix as he looked over the rail of the watchtower.

"Yep, they ain't pretty to look at, that's for sure." Fred smiled and reached Felix one of the sickles. "You ready for this?"

Felix grabbed the sickle and said, "Let's do this!"

Fred unlatched the door and started down toward the ground. He held the sickle in one hand as he held on to the ladder. Felix stepped on the ledge and closed the door; he started down after Fred with sickle in hand.

Fred glanced down. The two male ghouls were still unmindful of them, and Fred hoped it would stay that way. As they came within fifteen feet of the ground, one of the ghouls noticed them. It hissed and walked over to the ladder.

"I should've figured." said Fred as he stopped where he was.

"Now what Fred?" asked Felix as he looked down at Fred.

Fred watched the biter as it reached hands up toward him. The other biter noticed Fred and Felix; it ran over to join the other. Fred eased down a few steps. The biter's hands were only inches from Fred's feet. Fred leaned back from the ladder and kicked one of them in the face. The dead man stumbled back and groaned. Fred kicked the other in the face as well with the same results. Both biters came back and continued to reach for Fred's feet.

Felix gasped. "You just made them madder at us, Fred!" yelled Felix.

"I guess this will really tick 'em off then." Fred stepped down one more step; the biters grabbed Fred's ankle. The two held a tight grip on Fred's foot. He leaned down while holding on with one hand, raised the sickle high above his head and made a forceful swipe at one of the biter's arms. The sickle worked; the biter's arm fell to the ground beside of it.

"Whoo! Just like butter!" shouted Felix as he watched Fred take another swipe at the same biter's other arm.

The ghoul didn't seem to be affected by this; even though armless, it still moaned and hissed at Fred. Suddenly the other biter gave a strong tug on Fred's ankle, causing him to slip. He held on to the ladder and dangled for a moment.

Fred kicked at the ghoul's hands as it tried to grab his leg and take a bite. Fred forcefully kicked downward into its mouth. The impact caused its jaw to come unhinged and dangle. Fred took a swipe and cut off one of the arms. Fred wasn't struggling to hang on as much then; he took one more swipe and cut off the other arm from his ankle. Both biters still stood below them wanting a taste of their flesh and blood.

Fred repositioned himself on the ladder and leaned down. He took another hard swipe; this time at one of the necks. The sickle didn't completely go through; it only made it to the spine. Fred raised the sickle up and took a couple more swipes to its neck. Blood splattered with each hit. Finally the biter's head fell from its body.

"Whoa!" shouted Felix in amazement.

The biter fell to the ground beside of its head. Fred did the same with the last corpse, only this time he had to take two swipes to decapitate his foe.

"The neck's a little tough to cut through." said Fred as he stepped down a few steps and jumped to the ground. He looked down and saw both of the heads still moving their eyes around. "Well would you look a there!" he said to Felix.

Felix stepped off of the last step and walked over to look.

"They're eyes are still moving!" said Felix.

"I guess Nataleigh was right, you have to destroy their brain to kill them."

As Felix slowly moved his head up and down he said, "Guess so. We'd better get to moving before the rest of them head this way."

With a quick nod, Fred replied, "Let's move."

The two hurried over to the gate doors. Together they slid the blockade from the gate. As they began to pull the doors open both men saw a trio of biters down the street. The corpses didn't notice them right away.

As the men moved the doors, Ronald and the others could see inside the town. "C'mon boys, we've got some biters up there!" said Ronald as he looked ahead. Fred and Felix pulled both doors. As the doors swung apart the biters noticed the gate open. Instantly they charged.

"Here they come!" said Fred as he and Felix climbed in the wagon.

Ronald whipped the reigns and yelled, "He-yah!" The horses took off inside of town in a thundering fury. Dave struggled to stand up in the back with the scythe in his hands.

"Harvest time!" he yelled as the wagon approached

the trio of biters. Dave reared the long scythe back far behind his back. The horses galloped at a blazing speed down the street. Ronald steered the horses to run by the biters. Just as the wagon met with them, Dave fiercely swung the scythe with all of his might at the first ghoul's neck. With the force of Dave's swing, combined with the speed of the horses, the blade sliced completely through its neck. Everyone watched as the biter's body fell and rolled alongside the head.

"Whoa! Did you see that?" yelled Dave, excited his weapon worked. Everyone on the wagon was ecstatic. The other two biters shambled behind them, trying to catch up to the wagon. Ronald steered the horses around a curve and down a crowded street filled with the undead. As they passed, Dave swung like a madman, decapitating head after head. Nataleigh fired her gun at some of their pursuers. With each shot a corpse fell, occasionally two were hit by the scattering buckshot. Every biter in the street chased the wagon upon hearing it. Soon the group had a massive horde after them–everything was going just as they had planned.

"I could do this all day!" yelled Dave as he sliced the head off of another biter. The blade and nearly halfway down the handle of his scythe was covered in dark blood.

Ronald drove the wagon around another curve. Even more of the dead stumbled after the thundering steeds tearing through the town. Fred leaned up to talk to Ronald; he had to scream to be heard.

"The jailhouse is up ahead, we'll be far enough ahead to stop and drop me off! You keep driving around; I'll get everyone ready to catch the wagon. It might take you a couple of trips around, so don't worry if you don't see anybody outside on your first pass."

"Alright Fred! We'll be watching for you!" replied Ronald.

Fred patted Ronald on his shoulder. "Just stay far enough from them to give us some time to get everybody on; don't get too far from them though!" explained Fred.

With his eyes concentrated on the road in front of them, Ronald yelled, "I gotcha, Fred!"

They came around the final curve just before the jailhouse. Only a couple of biters was down the street in front of them. As Ronald brought the horses to a stop the two ghouls quickly approached them. Nataleigh shot one in the head and Fred shot the other with his pistol as he jumped down from the wagon.

"Go, go!" yelled Fred as the monstrous riot of the dead came down the street. Ronald had the horses moving again as Fred pounded on the door. At first no one answered, the mob was getting close. Fred pounded on the steel door once again.

"Hey!" He fired two shots to bring down a couple of the leading biters. "Open the door!" He pounded on it again. The dead were only two buildings away. Fred fired another shot. "Open the door!" he screamed.

Finally the door swung open just as the horde reached the building next to the jailhouse. Fred ducked inside and helped slam the door shut. Sid was the one who opened the door. Everyone was very glad to see Fred and celebrated his return.

"You're early, Fred! We weren't expecting you back so soon." said Sid as he patted Fred's back. "You look a little flustered."

"Yeah, nothing like a mob of hungry biters coming after ya to get the blood pumping." said Fred as he tried to regain his composure.

"Did everything go okay?" asked Silvia.

Fred was careful not to tell anything that went wrong to keep an argument from starting. He knew that every second from then on was precious. "We've got a little change in the plan, but I'll tell you about it on the wagon, I need you, Sheriff Hansen, and Octavia to come with me. Rusty and Bella, you two stay here with the kids and shut the door back."

Concerned, Sid asked, "What's going on, Fred?"

"We need you three to help push a boulder in front of the entrance after all the biters are in." explained Fred.

"A boulder?" asked Sid.

Fred could hear the gunshots and galloping horses coming back around the corner. "I'll explain it in a minute. We gotta move!"

Hesitant, Silvia and Octavia came to the door. Sid was ready to go. Rusty hurried near the door and said, "Good luck."

With a very worried look, Sid replied, "Thanks. I've got a feeling we're gonna need a little luck."

Fred opened the door and looked out to see Ronald and the others approaching them in the wagon.

"Everybody get on the wagon! Hurry!" said Fred as he motioned for the three to go out of the door. Ronald brought the wagon to a stop in front of the jailhouse. He stood and helped his wife on the seat next to him. Dave, Felix, and Nataleigh were in the back and helped Octavia up on the wagon. The hungry horde closed in on them fast. Sid climbed in the wagon. He reached his hand down and helped Fred on the wagon.

"Everybody's in!" yelled Fred.

Rusty slammed the steel door shut once again. Ronald cracked the reigns and they were on their way around the town again to make sure all of the biters were after them. The ride was very bumpy and unsteady. Dave sat down with his scythe; they weren't driving past anymore of the dead. The monsters were behind the wagon, chasing like blood-thirsty animals on the hunt.

Sid looked to Fred and asked, "What changed, Fred?"

"There's no exit."

Sid's eyes widened. "What do you mean there's no exit? What happened to it?"

"The roof collapsed near it."

"So what's the plan now?" asked Silvia as she was turned around in the front seat.

Fred looked around at the three that just joined them. Everyone else on the wagon looked ahead. "We're driving around to get the attention of every biter in town. We're still gonna be leading them to the mine. We'll be far enough ahead of them to be able to stop at the entrance. I'm getting off and you guys are gonna drive on around to the ledge above the entrance. You guys will lay low till I get their attention and run inside. They all should follow in after me."

They were confused by Fred's plan once he said this. They all continued to listen, thinking Fred must have something else up his sleeve. "Once they're all in, there's a path that leads straight down to the entrance from the ledge above. One person will have to drive the wagon back down the road to pick up the others while they push the boulder in front of the entrance to close it off so none of the biters will get back out. You'll need to hurry to do this because you gotta be far away when the explosion happens." Fred had a lump in his throat as he finished explaining. "Hopefully that'll be the end of this."

Nataleigh watched Fred as he talked. She turned away. Tears began to stream down her cheeks. Silvia and Octavia traded wide-eyed glances. Silvia then looked at Ronald, expecting an explanation from him.

Sid tightly closed his eyes and shook his head. "Hold on a second, Fred." He thought maybe he'd missed something. "I didn't hear the part where you get yourself out of there before the mine explodes."

Fred gave Sid a stern look as he said, "There ain't a

part like that." All eyes were on Fred.

Ronald yelled, "The gate is up ahead! Do you think we need to make another trip through?"

"No, we should be good! Let's get to the mine!" replied Fred as he looked up to see the gate.

Sid responded, "Make another trip through town, Ronald!"

Fred looked at Sid shocked. "Sid!" He turned his head and yelled back to Ronald, "Ronald take us to the mine, that's all of them!

"I said make another trip!" argued Sid. Fred looked at the sheriff with a frustrated gaze. "I'm the sheriff, Fred. Whatever I say goes in this town."

Ronald steered the horses back down the first street again. Sid wanted answers.

"Fred you ain't gonna go in there and blow yourself up!"

Fred gritted his teeth. "We ain't got no other choice! I've already argued about this enough! This was my idea to lead them inside this way and I won't stand by and let anybody else do it! Now, I'm done talking about it!" Octavia sat quietly as she watched Fred stare at Sid. Silvia glanced back to Ronald, who kept his eyes on the road ahead of them. Felix and Dave stayed quiet and watched the buildings pass by. No one wanted to see Fred die, but they knew he was right–someone had to make the ultimate sacrifice in order to get rid of the biters.

Sid just couldn't stand it; he didn't want his friend to lose his life like that. The people on the wagon was silent as it thundered through the street again, everybody felt the same about Fred, but they all knew he wouldn't have it any other way. As they all sat in the back, they watched the dead chasing them. Each person there recognized most of the faces in the crowd of flesh hungry beasts. The people they once knew; friends, and family that were no longer the same as they once were a day before. Never could any of them have imagined in their worst nightmares that this would have happened. Their lives had been torn apart, and their worlds were turned upside down.

Octavia looked at the faces of many of the people who she attended church with every Sunday. She thought of how her daughter would never know the kindness those people showed her during the days after her husband died years ago.

Felix too felt a sense of loss as he thought about the day he first came to Hazel and how the people shambling after them were so accepting of him. It was the only place that he and his family had ever felt comfortable to live without having to face the mindless ridicule from others for being black.

Dave looked out at and saw the people he had known his entire life. He was born and raised in Hazel. Hazel was his home, and everyone in that hungry mob was like a member of his family. Everything was going to be different from there on out.

The longer Sid looked at the mindless monsters, the angrier he became. They took everything he ever cared about from him. Soon he would lose a dear friend as well. "Fred, you can't do this." Tears swelled in his eyes. Fred just looked at him with a hint of sympathy. "Let me do it."

"Sid, no. I'm not gonna let you. These people need their Sheriff. Especially now, more than ever!"

Sid gave Fred a very sympathetic look. "Fred, let me do this for my town! If they need their Sheriff then let their Sheriff do this for them." Sid could barely hold back his emotions as his bottom lip started twitching. He wanted so badly to take Fred's place. "Fred, I want to do this for my family the most! Those things took my wife and son from me, and I want nothing more than to kill every last one of them!"

Fred's heart sank. He glanced at the corpses behind the wagon, then back to Sid. He had never thought of it like that. Fred let out an aggravated sigh as he shook his head. He was beginning to understand why Sheriff Hansen wanted to take his place. It would be his revenge for his family. "Sid. I just–I don't know." Fred looked down and the weathered boards of the wagon.

"Fred look at me! I want this for them." He paused. "There wasn't anything I could do for them before, but this time is different. I can now."

Fred looked into Sid's eyes and saw the desperation he held in his soul.

Sid continued, "This is the only thing that matters to me now, Fred. I know you can relate to this feeling. This want that is inside of me. It's killing me!" The sheriff patted his chest. "All I want is to avenge my family! Please Fred. This is my only chance to do that for them."

Fred rubbed his forehead as he looked up at the blue sky. He took in a deep breath and tasted the dirt that filled the air. Fred could no longer argue and knew this would eat at Sid for the rest of his life; Fred struggled with the same feelings since his parents were murdered. Fred nodded and looked at Sid. "Alright. If this is what you really want."

Sid's mood changed dramatically. The sheriff had that same spark in him Fred saw the first day he met the lawman; back when Sid joined his posse to hunt down the men that killed Fred's parents. Sid reached out his hand. "You're a good friend, Fred. Thank you." Fred tightly shook Sid's hand. The wagon neared the gate again.

"Get to the mine, Ronald. It's time!" yelled Sid with a smile. The wagon flew through the gate.

The view looking behind them was amazing. Every

visitor from the day before and every citizen of the town that had turned were right behind them in a cloud of dust. Their moans and hisses could still be heard above the bumping and squeaking of the wagon, and the galloping hooves of the horses.

They were about halfway to the hill leading up to the mine when Sid announced, "Just so everyone knows, after this, I will be stepping down as Sheriff. I think we need to appoint a new sheriff now to take my place. I want to nominate Fred Douglas."

A smile grew across Felix's face. Dave and Octavia nodded. Ronald looked back and said, "I think that's a good idea."

Fred was surprised. "Hold on now, people. I never said I would accept."

"C'mon, Fred! Everybody agrees with me. Like it or not this is the majority of the town right here in this wagon." commented Sid.

Nataleigh spoke up with a huge smile on her face, "Do it, Fred! You'd make a great sheriff."

Ronald glanced back for a moment and added, "She's right Fred; you've helped this town more than you'll ever know already. Just imagine what you could do as sheriff."

"I don't know." Fred was always afraid of the backlash most people got after becoming Sheriff.

Sid added, "Fred, you've got nothing to worry about. You're already a proven leader."

Hesitantly, Fred thought to himself for a moment, "How am I gonna ever help these people rebuild Hazel after this?"

Felix spoke up, "I'm for it! I don't think there's one of us that ain't."

Fred looked around the wagon and saw the hope in each person's eyes. He thought, "Who am I to take this from them, Lord?" Fred felt a calmness take over his heart. He nodded. "Alright. I'll do it."

Silvia and Ronald looked at each other and smiled.

Sid shook Fred's hand again and said, "You're gonna do just fine, old buddy."

"Thanks, Sid." sheepishly replied Fred.

The wagon neared the top of the hill; the mine was just a hundred feet away. Everyone was filled with sorrow, but felt happy for Sid at the same time. They all understood this is what he truly wanted.

Fred realized there wasn't much time left and he needed to explain everything to Sid. "Listen Sid; just go straight through the mine. There ain't no turns to take, just a straight shot to the detonator. They've got torches lit inside along the walls to help you see in there. You'll come inside a huge cavern and it's gonna be stacked to the gills with dynamite. The detonator is in the back of the room. You can't miss it."

Sid nodded. "Alright, I'll hold off as long as I can without setting it off." He patted Fred's shoulder. "You make sure you get everybody out of here, Fred. And you take care of yourself."

Fred smiled, "I will, Sid. Thank you for what you're doing."

"No, thank you for this, Fred. It means everything to me."

"I know it does," Fred said as the wagon slowed down.

Once the wagon came to a stop, Sid jumped off.

Dave gazed at Sid. "Goodbye Sheriff. You'll be always be remembered."

Tears flowed down Octavia's face as she watched Sid wave to everyone. "Thank you."

The biters could be heard making their way up the hill.

"Goodbye everybody." said Sid.

Everyone waved as the wagon moved away. Ronald

drove the horses up the road that lead to the ledge on top of the mine entrance. Once the wagon was out of sight, Sid turned to face the horde. He had waited only a minute when the first of the dead appeared at the hilltop. They seemed lost at first.

He waved his arms and screamed at the biters, "Hey! Come on!"

They saw him and shuffled toward him. The entire mob seemed to attack like a wolf pack.

"I'm coming, Donna." He turned and disappeared into the darkness of the mine.

* * *

Fred and the others reached the ledge. Ronald stopped the horses away from the edge to avoid being spotted by the biters. They heard the frenzied mass right below them. Fred jumped down.

"Silvia, you care to drive the wagon back down?" he asked.

"Sure." she replied as Ronald handed her the reigns.

"Everybody else come with me. Stay low, they're all still running inside." explained Fred. They crept to the edge to peek over.

"Wow!" whispered Felix as he saw the dead flowing into the mine like a river. They waited a moment as the last of the monsters ran inside. Fred motioned for Silvia to go.

"C'mon," whispered Fred. He ran down the steep path to the mine entrance. Everyone followed him to the bottom. Once there, they all gathered around the large boulder that sat at the end of the path. Each person pushed against the massive rock with all of their might. It budged a little, finally; making short strides to the entrance.

Silvia arrived at the entrance with the wagon. The boulder was nearly in place. She climbed down and ran over to help. Everyone struggled to push the boulder the last few inches it needed to go. The rock grinded against the sandstone entrance. Dust floated into the air as everyone's feet slid as they struggled against the sheer weight of the rock. At last, the extra help paid off. The boulder was in place and completely sealed off the entrance.

Fred waved his hand to everyone and yelled, "Everybody go!" They all scattered and ran back to the wagon. Ronald climbed back to the driver's seat and helped Silvia back on. Everyone else piled in the back.

Ronald let out a powerful "He-yah!" and the horses galloped away at full speed.

Octavia dusted off her dress and asked, "Even with them sealed in there when the dynamite goes off, is that gonna be enough to stop them?"

Fred coughed and said, "I hope so."

Everyone's eyes were on the mine as they reached the bottom of the hill.

Nervously Fred muttered, "C'mon, Sid." as he watched.

A few moments later the group was nearly back to the gate. Everyone watched anxiously as those last moments seemed to pass by like an eternity. Finally, a sudden deafening boom blasted out. A gigantic orange and red fireball erupted from the mine. The horses stopped; they were spooked and began bucking. The earth shook for a few moments as the flames stretched higher and higher into the sky. Everyone began shouting and cheering as the fireball was chased away by an enormous black cloud of smoke.

Ronald shouted, "He did it! Sheriff Hansen actually did it!" He stood up with his ecstatic wife. He wrapped his arms around Silvia and gave her the biggest hug and kiss he ever gave her. Everyone celebrated and sang for joy; their plan pulled through.

Fred and Nataleigh embraced each other.

"He did it, Fred!" said Nataleigh with her arms wrapped around Fred's waist and her head against his chest. Fred wrapped his arms tightly around her as he replied,

"Sid saved us all."

Chapter 16

"There they are!" yelled Bella as she was looking out of the jailhouse window. "They're all back!" She started clapping and laughing.

"Is it safe to go out there?" asked Rusty. He was over by Sid's desk playing with the two kids. Both children were lit up with glee as well.

"I don't know." Bella started waving at everyone through the window. Suddenly she realized someone was missing. "Rusty, Sheriff Hansen isn't with them."

Rusty stood from the chair and walked over to his wife. He peered out and scanned the group. "You don't think something has happened to him, do you?"

She put a hand to her mouth and said, "Oh goodness, I hope not."

Ronald saw the Martins looking out of the window and flagged them to come out.

"It must be okay to go out!" said Bella.

"Well c'mon!" said Rusty as he quickly walked to the door, moved the blockade, and opened the door. The kids ran outside to the wagon as the Martin's stepped out of the door.

Ronald stopped the horses and jumped off of the wagon. He helped Silvia down from the wagon. They were greeted by their son Michael. Ronald scooped his son up in his arms and held him tight. Octavia jumped down and ran to her daughter. It was a very happy reunion for them as they hugged and kissed.

Everyone else slowly got off of the wagon. Fred helped Nataleigh down.

"Sheriff Hansen didn't make it, did he?" asked Rusty.

Fred shook his head as he said, "No, he didn't. The change in the plan that I was talking about earlier was that the roof had collapsed near the exit of the mine. There was only the one way inside. Ronald, Dave, and Felix went ahead and set everything up in case we needed to finish the plan. The detonator had to be placed inside the room with all of the dynamite. To start with, I was gonna be the one to set off the explosion; Sheriff Hansen had other plans."

"He sacrificed himself." commented Rusty with a very proud look on his face.

Fred nodded. "That's what he wanted, he wanted to avenge his wife and son, and save us all."

As Ronald held his family tight to his sides he said to Rusty, "We've got a new sheriff around here. Sheriff Hansen's last wish was to leave his duties to Fred."

Rusty smiled. "Well good! I've always said you'd make a swell sheriff, Fred!"

"Well thank you Mr. Martin, I've heard that a lot lately." said Fred as he looked at Nataleigh. She smiled and winked at him. "Excuse me, there's something I need to do." Fred climbed up in the back of the wagon and spoke up. "Everyone, let me have your attention for a moment." Everybody walked to the back of the wagon to listen to Fred. "This is a little informal, but that's just me. I'm not one that's been known to do things by the book." The small group gazed at Fred as he cleared his throat. "You've all lost loved ones and people you've known for a very long time over the past couple of days. I, too, said goodbye to a dear friend today. Sid Hansen. He will forever be known in Hazel as a man that in our greatest time of need stepped up to protect his citizens. I have never in my life seen that kind of courage in one man while in the face of danger. This just goes to show how selfless Sid was." He paused and he looked at everyone. Some were crying; others smiled. "On this day, I want you all to remember what he has done for us. And we will go on; we'll rebuild this town to what it was before this horrible disaster happened. We lost many people; people that were our neighbors, friends, and family. We will do this for them!"

The tiny group applauded.

Fred placed his hand on his heart. "I have been chosen to lead you during this time of healing. I swear, I won't let you down. I'll show the same devotion and strength that Sid showed us all today. This is my promise to you."

"We're glad to have you Fred." said Ronald. "I mean Sheriff Douglas!"

Fred shook his head. "Just call me Fred. I'd rather keep it that way." Felix and Dave nodded their heads. They knew every word that Fred spoke would be true. Ronald lovingly squeezed Silvia's shoulder. She placed her hand on his as she rubbed Michael's hair. Rusty put his arm around Bella and patted Octavia on the back. The group was filled with a new sense of hope and pride. A feeling they had all been lacking for quite some time.

"Now the tough work begins." said Fred as he took a deep breath. "We're gonna have to get this cleaned up. It ain't gonna be an easy job, but it's something we have to do."

"What are we gonna do with all of the bodies left in

town?" asked Dave.

Fred thought for a second. "I figure it will be a bad idea to bury them. There might be a chance the biters could come back to life again. After what I've seen in the past couple of days, I believe anything is possible. So I think it would be best if we burn the bodies." Fred could see the pain that was still burning inside their souls. Having to remove the bodies of people they once knew and loved would be hard for them.

Bella looked at the faces of the others around her. She too saw the despair that was written so plainly in their eyes. "I say we have a big dinner for everyone tonight. I know we've all lost people, but we're still here. We should still be thankful for that." She loved to cook big meals and found great joy in cooking for people she loved.

"I think that's a very good idea, Bella," said Fred. The group agreed. Fred knew it wasn't much, but maybe a dinner celebrating what they still have would be good for them.

"We'll go through town and make sure no biters were left alive. Once everything is cleared; me, Ronald, Dave, Felix, and Rusty will start the cleanup. The ladies can work together on the dinner."

"Let's get this done, I'm hungry." said Felix in an attempt to help lighten everyone's spirits.

"You heard the man!" said Fred with a laugh. "Let's get to it."

Fred hopped off of the wagon and everyone walked through their wrecked town. There weren't as many bodies as everyone first anticipated, they figured most of them had reanimated. They looked inside of each building and down every alley. Once everything was cleared and the town was considered safe, the women prepared a meal at Betty's restaurant fit for an army. The men began the cleanup. They rode through town and loaded the half-eaten bodies into the back of the wagon. Rusty drove while the others traveled by foot alongside the horses.

"Over there's one." said Ronald as he pointed at a body on the ground next to the mercantile.

The men walked to the corpse.

Dave shook his head as they approached it. "That's Jim Howard."

Ronald took in a deep breath and looked at Fred. "He worked with us for years. Jim wasn't married or anything, he moved to Hazel with just the clothes on his back."

Jim's body lay on the ground on his back. His lips were gone, revealing his chipped, red stained teeth. Blood matted his hair to his gunshot head. His brown shirt was tattered and barely hung on him. The bite mark that caused his transformation was visible on his chest.

Fred shook his head. "That's a shame."

Ronald agreed and said, "Let's get him loaded up." He walked to his head and grabbed his arms. Dave lifted the legs. The two packed Jim's body to the wagon. They swung the body a few times to help build enough momentum to throw it onto the pile of corpses already in the wagon. Jim made a dull thump when he landed onto the others.

Fred turned his head. The sight of the putrid corpses was more than he could bare. "Alright, I think that's gonna be all we can take on this load."

They took the bodies to a massive stack of large, burning logs they had built outside of the gates; no one wanted the pile of burnt bodies inside of town. The cleanup took a couple of hours to finish.

It was about midday, and Fred was tending to the fire as the others brought in the last load of bodies.

"This is the last of 'em." said Ronald as they approached the fire. The disturbingly pleasant aroma of the burning flesh filled the air.

"We've still got more cleaning to do in some of the buildings. There's a lot of blood." added Rusty.

"Thank you, guys. This is just unbelievable." said Fred as they all looked at the pile of bodies on fire.

Ronald and Felix packed the last two bodies off of the wagon and heaved them into the flames. Ashes and smoke rose into the air once the bodies landed inside the inferno.

"It's just such a shame," Rusty quietly said.

Fred slowly nodded. "Yeah it is."

Ronald and Felix walked back over to Fred and Rusty.

"That does it for the bodies, though. At least that's done." said Ronald.

"I'm glad it's over!" commented Felix.

Fred had a puzzled look on his face. He made sure to watch the bodies carefully. "Hold on a minute. Are you guys sure that was all of them?"

"Yeah, we went back through every building before we brought those last two." replied Ronald confidently.

Fred stood there for a second. "There's still one more. I've been watching for it."

The others looked at each other confused.

"There's no way, Fred. The town is clean of them." said Ronald.

Fred turned and started walking back to the gate.

"Don't worry about it, I'll take care of it," he calmly said. The four men stood there as they watched Fred walk through the gate.

"What's he up to?" asked Ronald as he looked at the others.

"I don't know. Did we really forget any?" asked Dave. He continued to watch Fred walk away.

Ronald replied, "No." He followed Fred to see where the new sheriff was going. The others followed.

Fred walked down the street and around some

buildings. He crossed the street and went into the jailhouse. Fred walked over to the keys that hung on the rusty nail in the far wall. He flipped through the three keys and examined each of them. He found the one he was looking for and walked to the second cell door. Just as Fred inserted the key, Ronald and the others appeared.

"Fred," softly said Ronald. "We already got Doctor Richards' body out of there."

Fred didn't say anything. He turned the key and opened the squeaky cell door. Fred walked inside and stood there as he looked over the blood-covered floor; he saw the pile of black, blood-soaked rags lying there in the corner. Slowly he took a few steps toward the pile. Then Fred carefully reached down and began to grasp what was left of the black jacket. He suddenly yanked the jacket from the floor to reveal a horrid sight. The other men gasped at what they saw.

A mangled flesh and bare boned torso lay on the ground. It was Wellman. Red eyes rolled around looking at Fred then at the men standing at the door; his mouth moved up and down as he moaned. He couldn't move because all that was left was merely his chest and head; Dr. Richards had nearly devoured the entire body. It was one of the more gruesome carcasses they'd seen during the cleanup; a bust carved by the gnawing teeth of the undead.

Fred grinned as he looked down at Wellman. "Well imagine that, boys! Wellman here is hungry!" he said as he looked over at the disgusted men standing in the doorway. "But I guess there's some things that'll never change." Fred looked back down at what was left of Wellman and added, "He's lost a little weight, though."

Fred raised the jacket up and looked at the sheriff's badge attached to it. He unpinned the badge from Wellman's jacket and examined it for a moment. It was a little dirty so he found a clean spot on the jacket to wipe it off. Fred tossed the rag over in the cell's corner and pinned the badge on his shirt. He straightened the badge and said, "Let's see, where did I leave off the other day?" He paused. "Oh yeah." Fred knelt down next to Wellman. Wellman stretched his neck and chomped his teeth, trying to take a bite out of Fred. He moaned and hissed as his red eyes were locked onto Fred.

"Remember what that guy told you about me?" asked Fred as he looked into Wellman's hungry red eyes. Wellman moaned and chomped his teeth feverishly, desperate to take a bite of Fred's flesh.

"It was that part about me always getting my man." Fred grinned as he watched Wellman struggle.

Fred reached down and drew his pistol from its holster. He slowly put the end of the barrel just inches from Wellman's forehead–Wellman began straining for Fred's hand. "He was right." Fred was bursting with excitement as he began squeezing the trigger. He squinted his eyes and gritted his teeth as he watched Wellman chomp. Finally the hammer snapped forward as Fred fully squeezed the trigger.

Click.

Fred lowered his brow and looked down at the pistol. His feeling of excitement quickly left. Fred curiously examined his gun and was surprised to find empty shells in the cylinder. He rose back to his feet as he unloaded the bullets into his hand. While standing there with the empty shells in one hand and the pistol in the other, he looked down at Wellman who was still snapping. Fred shrugged his shoulders. He suddenly raised his foot up and stomped down on Wellman's forehead with the heel of his boot. Wellman's skull crunched as Fred's boot sank into it. Blood oozed from Wellman's head. Fred raised his boot out of Wellman's skull; Wellman was no longer moving. Fred held his foot up for a moment as he looked around. He turned it to the side and tried to wipe some of Wellman's brain matter off of his boot and onto the floor. Fred started walking toward the door as he continued to move his foot side-to-side trying to clean the mess on his boot as he walked. Fred looked up at the other men and said, "Okay. That's all of them now." The men smiled and patted Fred's shoulders as they walked to the cell to remove Wellman.

THE HEIST
(BONUS STORY)

THE HEIST

"Here, let me have a go at it for a while, Josiah." said Ronnie as he reached for the shovel in Josiah's blistered hands.

Josiah let out a long breath as he shoveled the last scoop of dirt and sandstone onto the pile on the surface.

"Whew," gasped Josiah while running his filthy fingers through his dark brown hair. He handed the shovel up to Ronnie, and climbed out of the chest-deep hole. He let his fatigued body fall to the ground a few feet away, right next to the spot his Winchester rifle and water canteen laid. "How much further do we got to go?"

Ronnie jumped into the hole and started digging at the dirt like a mad man. "It shouldn't be much further now." His huge arm muscles bulged as he tore chunk after chunk of earth from itself.

Josiah knew Ronnie was telling the truth once he saw the enormous vein start to protrude out the side of his bald head. Ronnie would never work himself that hard unless there was going to be a big payoff for it. There would indeed be a handsome reward once they had Minnie Cratchet's body dug up. She was the wife of the richest man in Whittlersfield, Sammy Cratchet. Word got around town that Sammy had her buried with a ridiculous amount of expensive jewelry on. Josiah and Ronnie were very eager to pay a visit to her grave.

Josiah uncorked the beat-up metal canteen and placed it to his dry lips at once. A rush of relief swam down his throat as he chugged the water as fast as he could. He then raised it high above him and poured the soothing liquid all over his sweaty head. As Josiah looked up, he noticed how dark the sky appeared. The moon and stars were nowhere to be seen across the vast nothingness above them.

"It sure is cloudy out tonight, ain't it?"

Ronnie, still hard at work digging scoop-by-scoop closer to their prize grunted, "Yep."

"Ya know, my grandpaw told me a story one time about nights like this." Josiah looked over at Ronnie in the grave. Dirt flew out of it at an impressive rate. "Used to creep me out when I was little."

He paused. "Still does."

"That so?"

"Yeah. He said when the nights are at their darkest like this, things of the devil come out to play. He swore he saw some of the craziest stuff around here at night time." Josiah picked the lantern up off the ground, held it high in the air, and looked around him.

"Josiah! Quit messin' around and keep that light shinin' over here! I can't see a thing I'm diggin' at!"

Josiah snapped back around and placed the lantern back where it was.

"Here!"

"Alright, keep it sittin' there! We ain't got time to mess around. There's probably just a few hours left till mornin' and we gotta get this done tonight." Ronnie struck at the ground again and continued digging even harder.

Josiah stood still for a moment as he watched Ronnie. He didn't want to do anything else to upset him. Suddenly Josiah felt a drop of water land on top of his head. "Uh oh."

Ronnie stopped digging as he looked up at the sky. "That's great. Just what we needed… rain!" He shook his head and drove the shovel into the ground.

The raindrops began falling faster and faster, until it became a steady drizzle. The light of the lantern flickered, and then disappeared. Ronnie cursed aloud.

"What do ya want me to do, Ronnie?"

Ronnie motioned his head to his side. "Get in here and help me dig!"

Josiah jumped into the grave with his back to Ronnie. He bent over and scratched at the dirt with his hands. The duo dug frantically, trying to reach Minnie's coffin in the dark. The rain soon turned the dirt into mud.

"I don't know if this is worth all of the trouble, Ronnie!"

A hollow thump came from the ground as Ronnie shoved the shovel into the ground. A grin crept across Josiah's face as he turned toward Ronnie.

"You're about to see my friend exactly how much this was worth it." Ronnie began laughing hysterically. He scraped the thin layer of mud and rocks away from the wooden coffin's top. "Dig around the sides!"

Josiah dragged his hands around the edge, making a small ditch around the sides. Ronnie pushed the sharp edge of his shovel between the lid and the wall of the coffin. Josiah held himself over it by placing both feet on opposite sides of the grave as Ronnie pried the lid off.

The putrid stench of rotting flesh immediately filled the air as Ronnie started to separate the lid from the wooden tomb. Josiah gagged as he held his nose.

"Oh Lord! I can't believe I let you talk me into this"

"Trust me buddy, its all gonna be worth it."

With one more hard push on the shovel, the lid quickly popped up and fell back down.

"Help me lift this outta here," said Ronnie as he threw the shovel up to the ground above. Both men grabbed one side of the lid and raised it above their heads. With a mighty shove, the lid landed topside up on the grass.

Ronnie lit a match and held his hand over it to shield it from the rain. Josiah looked down in disgust as Ronnie moved the match toward Minnie's rotten corpse. Most of the flesh on her face was rotted away, revealing the face bones of her skull. A little hair remained atop her head in sparse patches. Maggots scattered from her neck and from underneath the flower-pattern dress she wore as Ronnie moved the light down to reveal three gold necklaces resting on her chest.

"Oh yeah, there we go," said Ronnie as he moved his hand away from the flame. The light diminished, leaving them in darkness once again.

Ronnie struck another match and quickly moved it to her partially decayed hands. Minnie's fingernails were brown and chipped. Her left hand laid over her right. Josiah quickly noticed the gold wedding band on her ring finger, and other assorted diamond rings on the other fingers.

The rain quickly moved out just as Ronnie shook the match and threw it to the side.

Ronnie pointed up and said, "Go see if you can get that lantern lit again."

Josiah put his slender forearms on the grass at the grave's edge and pulled himself out. He turned and snatched the small box of matches Ronnie held in the air. After a few tries, Josiah had the lantern blazing. He grabbed it and held it over the grave for Ronnie to see. Minnie's rotten corpse looked even more gruesome in the luminous light. The cruel shadows accented her hollow eye sockets and rotten neck.

Ronnie bent over and started fidgeting with Minnie's decayed fingers. He slid four of the rings off with ease. Her left pinky rest on the edge of her right hand. It was bent and Ronnie struggled to remove the last ring from the stiff, curved finger.

"Why you stubborn little booger. Come off of there," said Ronnie. He twisted and tugged on the ring with futile results. Josiah could tell Ronnie was getting very aggravated. Ronnie stopped and stood there for a second. "Well, there's more than one way to skin a cat." He forcefully grabbed her pinky and started to twist it.

Josiah cringed at the sound of Minnie's bone snapping apart.

Ronnie turned around with a giant smile on his face, holding Minnie's crumbling pinky between his thumb and index finger. "Looky here, Josiah! It looks like a wrinkled little caterpillar."

Josiah gritted his teeth and closed his eyes. "That's just sick."

All of a sudden, just up the hill, the two horses they rode to the gravesite began panicking. They were still tied to a couple of trees where they left them.

Josiah quickly turned the lantern toward the horses and held it up to see what was the matter. "What in the blazes is going on with them?" He squinted his eyes and moved his head side-to-side.

Ronnie peeked his head out of the grave and held his hand up, trying to block the glare of the lantern from his eyes. "I bet it's a pack of coyotes up there after them." He quickly reached down and tore the gold necklaces from Minnie's body. After stuffing them into his pocket, Ronnie jumped up and pulled himself out of the grave.

Josiah and Ronnie snatched their guns up from the

ground and ran toward the horses. Ronnie held his pistol in the air and fired two shots, hoping to spook the coyotes away.

"Get outta here you mangy devils!" he shouted.

By the time the men reached them, the horses were still screaming and bucking. Josiah ran around the horses with the lantern still held high and his rifle pointed in front of him.

"Go on! Get!" he screamed. He popped off a shot into the darkness, hoping to shoot one of them or at least scare them off. Josiah hung the lantern on a broken branch of the tree his horse was tied.

Ronnie was inspecting his horse's legs as he said, "Looks like they got Lady's leg pretty good."

Josiah hung his rifle on his shoulder and walked over to have a look at the horse's injuries.

"They sure did, didn't they?" Josiah gently touched Lady just above a deep gash in her front leg. He looked up into Lady's eyes and patted her neck. "She's gonna be alright though, she's a tough girl."

Ronnie let out a heavy sigh. "We best be movin' on outta here." He untied Lady from the tree.

Josiah raised his eyebrows. "Ronnie, ain't we even gonna cover Minnie back up first?"

"Ain't got time, Josiah. We better go before it gets light out."

Josiah's mouth hung open. "We can't just leave her body like that! What if those coyotes come back?"

Ronnie shrugged his shoulders as he buckled his holster around his waist. "Oh well. That ain't our problem, now is it?"

Out of nowhere, a piercing screech came from the darkness close by in the forest. Josiah's blood ran cold as he ripped his rifle from his shoulder. Ronnie held his pistol out as he frantically looked around them.

"What was that," Ronnie whispered.

Josiah's heart felt like it was about to beat out of his chest. "Ronnie, I know you probably ain't in the mood to hear another of my grandpaw's stories, but he told me a story about that very sound."

"Shut up, Josiah! I don't wanna hear another one of your grandpaw's drunken tales. There's somethin' in them woods right now." Ronnie pointed his gun and fired another shot. "Get outta here!"

The squall unexpectedly echoed through the forest once again.

"I'm telling you, he knew what he was talking about! Didn't you just hear that thing? It was real now wasn't it?"

Out of the corner of his eye, Josiah saw a white figure scurrying on its hands and feet toward them. He turned to face the pale-skinned beast. Its wide eyes faintly glowed in the lantern's light, and in the middle of the humanoid face were two slender nostril holes. The hairless creature wailed as it rushed toward them, revealing the long, pointed teeth inside its mouth. Josiah noticed the creature's lean body and wondered how it could move at such a blazing speed. He raised his rifle at the monster and fired a shot. The creature abruptly darted to its left, back into the cover of darkness.

"Dear Lord, what was that thing," yelled Ronnie. Beads of sweat glistened all over his face and head. His eyes were locked in a panicked stare toward the creature's last whereabouts.

Josiah tried to calm his own nerves as he reloaded his Winchester.

"My grandpaw was right, Ronnie!" He snapped the gun ready and held it against his cheek. "He called that thing a Deadin!"

"How do you even know that's what he was talking about?"

Just then, the Deadin let out another high-pitched wail somewhere in the darkness that surrounded them. Josiah and Ronnie flinched.

"That's one reason right there And didn't you see the way it looked? It's exactly like he told me."

Josiah followed the sound of rustling leaves and snapping twigs with the end of the gun barrel until the sound came to a sudden stop. Ronnie froze while pointing his gun at the shadows.

"You see it anywhere?" His eyes glanced back and forth.

Josiah held still, listening for the Deadin.

"I'm not sure, I think it's over there," he whispered.

Branches started to move in the tree behind them, and before either of the men had time to react the Deadin grabbed Ronnie's leg. Ronnie screamed as the Deadin growled and sunk its dagger-like teeth into his thigh. He immediately pointed and shot his .45 at the monster. It squealed in agony as a burst of solid black blood sprayed from its boney back. The Deadin let go, but only for a moment. It pounced forward and resumed the attack on Ronnie's leg.

Josiah was afraid to shoot the Deadin; he worried the buckshot would hit Ronnie. He rushed at the Deadin and kicked it right under the ribs, knocking it back. The monster swung its long claws at Josiah. The beast barely missed slicing Josiah's stomach as he jumped backwards. Spotting his chance, Josiah fired a wad of buckshot at the Deadin's head. The back of its skull exploded in a mist of dark blood and brain matter. The ferocious monster's body fell limp and collided on the ground.

Josiah looked the monster over while still aiming his rifle. It appeared to be around five-feet tall. The Deadin's hands had three fingers and a thumb, each with sharp, pointed claws. The skin that covered its body was so pale, dark veins could be clearly seen. Josiah saw the blood smeared all around its mouth, and then glanced over at Ronnie.

"You alright?"

He lowered the gun and ran to his friend's side. The Deadin had torn a large chunk of muscle from the back of Ronnie's leg. Josiah felt dizzy once he saw Ronnie's femur deep inside the wound.

"Oh no." Josiah looked at Ronnie's pale face. "I've gotta get you back to Doctor Samson."

Ronnie was loosing a lot of blood. He reached into his pocket and held out the necklaces and rings.

"Here. You hold on to these."

Josiah took the ball of jewelry and walked to his horse, Hector to put it in the small cloth bag he had tied to the saddle. As Josiah pulled the bag open, he heard the unexpected screech of a Deadin, followed by Ronnie screaming for dear life. Josiah immediately turned and saw a Deadin on Ronnie's back. Ronnie tried to reach the nimble monster over his shoulders, but couldn't. The beast had its clawed toes dug deep into his sides. Ronnie cried out as he stumbled around, wrestling to get it off. With its mouth wide open, the Deadin reared its head back and sank its teeth into Ronnie's neck. It growled and hissed as it tore the flesh from his body.

Suddenly another Deadin bounded out of the darkness like some mutated cat. It helped the other Deadin bring Ronnie to the ground and tear into him at once. Josiah couldn't believe his eyes as he continued to watch more and more Deadin swiftly emerge from the shadows. They soon began attacking Ronnie's horse, Lady as well. The awful sounds of screeching Deadin, along with Ronnie and Lady's cries as they were being eaten alive filled the night air.

Josiah knew there was nothing he could do to save

his partner. The only thing left to do was get out with his own life while he could. He grabbed the lantern, untied Hector from the tree and mounted him.

"He-yah," he yelled as he kicked the horse.

By then, ten Deadin had huddled around Ronnie and Lady's bodies. Josiah insisted Hector go faster as he continued to whip the reigns as they started down the muddy trail. Hector galloped down the trail at a furious speed. Josiah held the swinging lantern up as Hector maneuvered through the winding turns. Josiah had a hard time seeing where they were going, but placed all trust into his mighty steed.

A chill ran down Josiah's spine when he heard the wicked shriek of a Deadin close behind him. He turned to see a lone Deadin running on its hands and feet chasing Hector through the trail. Out of sheer terror, Josiah tossed the lantern at his pursuer. It smashed in a small ball of fire on the ground in front of the Deadin. The creature jumped to the side to avoid the fireball. It was gaining ground on them. Josiah reached over his shoulder to grab his Winchester. As soon as Josiah readied his gun against his shoulder to take aim, he was knocked from his horse by a low hanging branch. He hit the ground with a great impact.

As Josiah laid there in the mud, stunned and in pain, he listened as the sound of Hector's thundering hooves and the wails of the Deadin faded into the distance. The moon shined through the clouds, providing a small amount of light. It was just enough for Josiah to see his surroundings. Once Josiah could no longer hear Hector, he struggled to crawl off the trail with his rifle to the other side of a large tree. Once there he leaned his back against the trunk of the tree. Josiah struggled to catch his breath after having the wind knocked out of him.

Just as Josiah felt a brief sense of safety, he heard the

sloppy sounds of bare feet beating against the muddy trail coming toward him. The wet slaps were in a rhythm of four beats. He tightly clinched the rifle in his hands, knowing his one remaining shell could take care of just one of those horrid creatures. Josiah sat still as he listened to the creature get closer. He held his breath as the foot steps galloped past him.

Josiah slowly exhaled a sigh of relief. He became so overwhelmed with emotions, tears started to swell up in his eyes. He closed his eyes as he began sobbing uncontrollably. He grieved for his friend and silently asked for forgiveness for the horrible things he had done that night.

All of a sudden, Josiah could feel his heart stop as he felt a few gentle puffs of air on his face, accompanied by a sniffing sound. He opened his eyes to discover a Deadin looking him in the eyes. Josiah panicked and did the first thing that came to his mind. He shot his final bullet without aiming it whatsoever. The buckshot burst into the sky from the barrel. The Deadin pinned Josiah against the tree and tore into his throat with its razor sharp teeth. Blood gushed from Josiah's mouth as three other Deadin joined in. Each of them tore his body apart in a feeding frenzy. He could hear more Deadin screeching as they made their way to him. Josiah watched the twenty or so Deadin surround him, fighting for any morsel of his own body. At last, the searing pain of claws penetrating his skull put an end to Josiah's final heist as a Deadin ripped his head from his shoulders

END

If you enjoyed the short story, "**The Heist**", try Jason Thacker's horror short story collection "**KING AND OTHER CHILLING TALES**".

KING AND OTHER CHILLING TALES is a collection of six adrenaline pumping horror short stories from author, Jason Thacker. In this collection you'll walk alongside the legions of the walking dead, and the fierce monsters of myth that roam the mysterious forests of Appalachia. Monsters such as the vicious Mothman who's out for blood, and a frightening Wampus Cat on a deadly prowl in one man's own backyard. This little book will keep you on the edge of your seat until the bitter end.

Jason Thacker was born in Pikeville, Ky and still resides in the beautiful mountains of Eastern Kentucky with his wife, Tiffany, and their two dogs, Rusty the Cairn, and Bella the Scottie. His first published work is "**The Hungriest Zombie**" in the anthology "**FIRST TIME DEAD 2**" from May December Publications. Jason has published two other short stories and also a short story collection titled, "**KING AND OTHER CHILLING TALES**". Jason is currently at work on many upcoming projects, so keep an eye out for what's to come in the future.

You can keep in touch with Jason on Facebook at

http://www.facebook.com/authorjasonthacker

or follow him on Twitter at

@jason_thacker

Stay up to date with his latest projects or browse his website at:

http://jasonthacker.wordpress.com

Contact Jason directly at **jt4287@hotmail.com**.

http://www.scribeimagery.com

- Book Layout
- Cover Design
- Book Trailers
- Audio Compilation
- Website Design
- Photography
- Imagery
- Bulk Scanning and Digital Document Archival

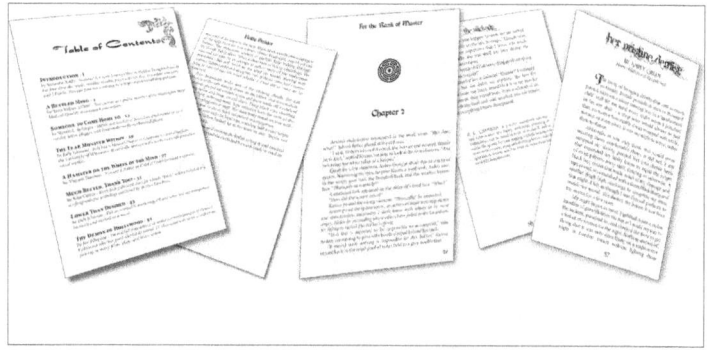

www.ingramcontent.com/pod-product-compliance
Lightning Source LLC
Chambersburg PA
CBHW070827180626
46818CB00001B/419